SHIFTERS

JESSICA'S STORY

ALLIE CARLSON

Shifters

Copyright © 2025 by Allie Carlson.

MILTON & HUGO L.L.C.
4407 Park Ave., Suite 5
Union City, NJ 07087, USA

Website: *www. miltonandhugo.com*
Hotline: *1- 888-778-0033*
Email: *info@miltonandhugo.com*

Ordering Information:
Quantity sales. Special discounts are granted to corporations, associations, and other organizations. For more information on these discounts, please reach out to the publisher using the contact information provided above.

Library of Congress Control Number:	2025917112	
ISBN-13:	979-8-89285-282-1	[Paperback Edition]
	979-8-89285-636-2	[Hardback Edition]
	979-8-89285-283-8	[Digital Edition]

Rev. date: 08/06/2025

For Larae, who gave me refuge when the library doors were closed,
and for Ira, whose feedback kept me on course.
I couldn't have done this without you.

We are Shifters.
Feared and shunned by society, we are outcasts. Our families disown us. Our friends ignore us. When we speak, the government silences us.
And when we disappear, no one bats an eye.
This is our story.

PROLOGUE

The Escape

The air reeked of blood and bleach.

Three girls—swift as shadows—darted down the corridor, flitting from one shadow to the next. One cradled a bundle of towels against her chest like a baby.

Pained screams echoed from deep in the building, broken up by sobs begging for release, for mercy—for death.

"This way," one girl hissed, jerking her head down another hallway. A solid metal door stood at the end.

We're going to make it.

They eased the door open.

Brrrraaaaang!

The alarm split through the air like a gunshot.

"*Run!*" one of them screamed.

They took off across the compound, heading for the gap in the fence they'd made on arrival. Guards poured from the exits. A hail of bullets burst around them as they ran.

"*Argh!*"

The one carrying the bundle screamed as blood burst from her thigh. The other two skidded to a stop and stared back in horror.

The tallest of the girls stepped between her injured friend and the guards. She snarled as her muscles rippled beneath her skin, and she fell to all fours. In her place stood a lioness, growling and prowling. She roared and swiped at the guards as they approached.

"Take her," the injured girl gasped. "Get out of here."

The remaining girl hunched down. Brown and white feathers sprouted from her skin, and a moment later a small bird of prey—an osprey—stood in her place. She grabbed the bundle in her talons and beat her wings frantically, struggling to get airborne with the extra weight. A bullet whizzed by her wing, missing her by centimeters. A guard rushed her as she took off. His fingers brushed her tail feathers.

Below, the lioness gave one final roar, then—the guns silenced her.

The osprey wheeled once overhead—helpless to save her friends— then turned and vanished into the night.

After the chaos, silence.

Two gurneys rolled down the corridor, wheels squeaking over bloodstained tile.

The first bore the lioness—now just a girl again, limp and pale, her skin marred with bullet wounds. They wheeled her through a steel door marked *"Autopsy."*

The second gurney turned a different corner. It went through another steel door with a name placard glinting on the wall: "Dr. I. Volkov, CEO."

She was still breathing.

And she was about to be introduced to her own personal hell.

Two Shifters in the Family

Dear Diary,

I'm seventeen today! Mom and Dad got me a nice wrist watch, gold with my initials behind the hands. Jess saved up her money and bought me this diary and a nice pen to write in it. The cover is leather, and the paper is good-quality heavy paper.

A scientist from the Shifter Rehabilitation Centre came to our school today. She explained the genetic differences between Shifters and Non-Shifters and some of the theories of why Shifters are the way they are. We were given a list of the symptoms to watch out for in the next year-ish. Stuff like muscle cramps, spasms, headaches, change in appetite, etc. I don't remember them all. She told us to keep an eye on our friends as well as ourselves and to report any suspicious behavior.

We saw a video of a lady who turned into a snake and a man who turned into an eagle. Then they were put next to the real animal, and we had to try and pick out which was the Shifter. It was almost impossible; they were so close. The one thing that stood out was the Shifter symbol that was branded on their neck. The scientist said it has to be a brand because things like tattoos are often lost under fur or scales. The brand is a scar, so it shows better when they're animals. The brand is an upside-down triangle with three lines that start in the middle and radiate out to the corners. Under the brand, a set of letters and numbers are tattooed.

I feel bad for them. The man and the lady in the video looked so sad. Mom and Daddy look down on them, but it's not their fault. They didn't ask to be born the way they are. I want to help them, but I don't know how.

I know! I'll become a scientist, like the lady at school today. I'll help find a cure.

I think Jess got caught climbing the old oak tree again 'cause I can hear Daddy yelling. Something about her "going to break her neck one of these days." He can yell all he wants, that won't stop Jess from climbing. That would be like trying to keep me from swimming.

Must run now, Mom is calling.

Love always,
Dani

~*~

"Jess? Are you still there?" Wyatt's voice pulled Jessica back to reality.

She closed the diary with a snap and dropped it on the bed.

Bringing the phone back to her ear, she sheepishly whispered, "Sorry. Yeah, I'm listening. I just spaced out there for a second." She didn't dare speak louder than a whisper. If her parents heard her, all their plans would be ruined.

"I was saying you should probably leave soon if you want to make it to the airport in time. The website says their next flight here is at 7:00 a.m."

"I know," Jessica sighed. "I hate that I have to sneak out this way."

"Babe, you know what they did to Dani when she got tested."

Jessica shivered, though the room was warm. She'd heard the rumors about the SRC, and she knew all too well what her parents were capable of.

"So it's about a two-hour flight. I'll be at the airport at nine to pick you up."

"I can't wait," Jessica whispered with a smile.

He'd only been gone a couple weeks, but it felt like a lifetime.

"Okay, you go get ready, or you'll never make it to the airport on time. I'll see you soon. I love you."

"I love you too," Jessica breathed. She waited till she heard the click of the line going dead before she put the phone down on her nightstand. She didn't dare take it with her on the off chance her parents actually decided to look for her.

She checked the clock on top of her dresser—2:00 a.m. Perfect. She fished for a small flashlight from under her pillow and clicked it on. The narrow beam shone across her bedroom as she quietly crept out of bed. Every creak of the floorboards was amplified in the silence of the early morning, and she kept stopping to listen for footsteps.

She opened her closet. Quickly and quietly, she pulled out a T-shirt and pulled it on. Over that she pulled on a long-sleeve shirt. Over that, a sweater. The nights had been cold lately, and it was a long walk to the airport. Wool socks and jeans finished her ensemble.

From under the bed, she fished out an old book bag. She fumbled around with the brown leather straps that were beginning to crack with age. Setting the bag on the bed, she shone the flashlight into it and quickly double-checked its contents. Passport. Money. Wallet. She patted each one nervously, sure she was forgetting something. She stuffed the diary into the bottom of the bag where it wouldn't get wet.

Satisfied she had what she needed, she closed the flap on the bag and buckled the straps again. Slinging the bag over her shoulder, Jessica crept to the window, still listening for her parents' approaching footsteps. She'd never been caught before, but tonight the stakes were higher than ever. Slowly and carefully, she pulled up the antique window, trying to keep the squeaks of the aged wood to a minimum. Inch by inch, she eased the window up, wiggling it through the stiff points in the frame. Halfway up, the window got stuck.

"You stupid piece of shit window!" Jessica whispered. She used every bit of her willpower to resist whacking it with her flashlight. The windows were ancient, tiny things that barely met the fire code. There was no way she'd fit through unless it was open all the way. She knew from experience that the window would let out a shriek of ungodly volume if she tried to force it up any further. Pulling the window back down would most likely result in the window slamming with a bang loud enough to wake the neighbors.

After letting out a slew of whispered curse words, she took a steadying breath and readied herself. The front door was her only other option. She crept as silently as possible out of her room and down the stairs. Every creak made her heart leap into her throat. Her mother's insomnia had gotten worse in the past three years, and she was hardly dressed to use a midnight pee as an excuse.

Jessica made it down the stairs before anything else went wrong. Pain lanced through her thigh, sharp and sudden. She stifled a cry and grabbed the wall to steady herself. Her muscles tightened around her knee, and she thought for sure it would end up dislocated. She clenched her jaw and hissed. Then, just as quickly as it came, the spasm passed. She gingerly bent her knee, then tested her weight on her leg. She listened intently. Nothing. Her parents hadn't heard her.

The flickering light of the living room television led her down the hall toward the door. As she got closer, her father's snores punctuated the news.

"Strictions come into ef—" *Snore.* "Day. Police anticip—" *Snore.* "Tests, which could eas—" *Snore.* "Lence. Please excer—"

Jessica peeked into the living room as she passed. There was her father, dead to the world in his recliner. Empty beer cans littered the coffee table. Three years had seen her father go from being a successful business owner to a shambling shell of his former self. The only reason his business hadn't completely gone under was his godsend of a manager who took over running it.

It was strange, Jessica mused as she eased the front door open, how someone could go from idolizing a person to feeling nothing but contempt for them. After all, his misery was all his own doing. *He* was the reason Dani was gone. *He* was the reason Jessica was leaving.

He'd never survive having two Shifters in the family—and Jessica wasn't about to wait around and watch it kill him.

~*~

The first time Jessica saw a Shifter in person she was six years old. It was summer, and the air hung hot and heavy over their neighborhood.

4

Most of the grown-ups retreated into the air-conditioned sanctuary of their house sand the kids to a creek in a nearby forest to splash around.

She and Dani were splashing in the shallows with five other kids, throwing water at each other and squealing as kids do. They were soaked to the bone and having the time of their lives when the rustling of leaves stopped them mid-splash.

Through the branches, a huge creature emerged. It was enormous, with shaggy dark-brown fur. A ginormous set of antlers sat on its head. Dani looked up the creature later that day and told Jessica it was a moose. Whatever that was.

The moose snorted and stomped a hoofed foot, shaking its huge head at them. The kids screamed and took off toward home. Jessica, the youngest at the time, fell behind. In a panic, she scrambled up a tree, convinced the moose was going to eat her.

When she looked back however, she watched with abject curiosity as the moose shrank and twisted into a human form. The now-naked man stooped down and took a big drink from the creek. He splashed the cool water on his face and scrubbed behind his ears.

He disappeared a few minutes later, shifting back into the dreaded moose form and ambling back into the forest.

It took Dani thirty minutes and the promise of a chocolate bar from the store to convince Jessica to come down from the tree.

~*~

It was the most shameful thing, to be related to a Shifter. Other than being a Shifter yourself, of course. That mindset had been drilled into Jessica's head her entire childhood.

"They're worse than animals," her father loudly declared anytime they were brought up. Her mother always nodded her head vigorously in agreement. Back then her parents had the pride of being able to claim that their bloodline was Shifter free for three whole generations. Nothing mattered more to the Normals than their blood status, and the less your family were associated with the Shifters, the better.

Jessica was coming to the part of her journey that scared her the most: the checkpoint to get into the ghetto where the Shifters lived. The airport she was going to was on the other end of the ghetto. It wasn't illegal for her to enter the ghetto, but the less people who saw her, the better.

She stopped as soon as the checkpoint came into view. She needed a way in. She took in the landscape, searching for an alternate route.

Just when things began to look hopeless, Jessica saw her route: a clump of trees near the wall. Jessica ducked between the houses and crept behind the wooden fences that encircled the backyards. Coming to the end of the last fence, she took a chance and dashed the last few feet to the clump of trees. As soon as she was under the canopy, she ran to the tree nearest the wall and shimmied up.

The bark of the tree was rough—rougher than what she was used to anyway. The branches of her tree at home had been worn smooth from years of her climbing the same routes. For a brief, disorienting moment, the danger ceased to exist. A familiar thrill fluttered through her chest. Up here, in the branches, she felt safe, felt at home.

Once she was safely off the ground, she stopped and listened. No shouting. No footsteps. No alarms. The rustle of leaves.

Jessica breathed deep, then carefully picked her way to a larger branch close to the wall. She clambered out as close to the end of the branch as she thought could hold her weight. The branch swayed under her weight. Five feet still separated her from the top of the wall. Jessica steadied herself, then leapt.

Her toes hit the wall, slipped. Her stomach slammed into the concrete edge, driving the air from her lungs. She clung to the wall desperately, wheezing, nails scraping for purchase. With a heave, she pulled herself up and over.

Her feet hit the ground with a soft *thud*.

She paused, listening intently. Silence. No alarm was raised. No guards came running.

She made it.

~*~

Jessica sank down on the bench at the bus stop. Her lungs still burned as she gasped for breath. Her legs ached, and her toes had their own pulse.

She looked around while she rested. Now miles from the safety of her gated suburb, the divide between Normals and Shifters was evident. The ghetto where the Shifters lived stood between the airport and her old neighborhood. In the gray predawn light, Jessica could see makeshift shelters littering the alleyways between the buildings. A stench wafted into the streets, trapped by the tall buildings that surrounded them. It was the smell of industry and human filth. The Shifters shambling about those alleys had a feral look to them. Most bore the brand that identified them as Shifters. She'd known that this was here. But actually seeing it... Jessica pushed down the feelings that swirled in her gut.

Jessica shivered. She was suddenly aware of how out of place she was with her clean clothes and brand-name sneakers. She stood up with renewed energy. Her legs still ached, but something told her it was time to go.

"Just a little further, and then we'll be on our way," Jessica said, spurring herself forward.

She marched on. A bit further on, Shifters started trickling out of the run-down apartment buildings. Though somewhat less disheveled than the alley Shifters, they still had a wild look about them.

These were the factory workers. This much she knew. Many Shifters opted to work in the factories because they paid their workers in room and board. She could remember her parents talking about it with their neighbor when she was younger. The neighbor had just found out their son was a Shifter, and they were worried about how he would survive on his own. Shifters weren't permitted to live in her neighborhood.

Her parents doled out the fake sympathy, reassuring them that the boy would be fine.

"Oh, Barbara, he's a strong young man. He can get a job in one of the factories there," her mother soothed.

"That's right," her father had chimed in. "The factory workers get free housing and three square meals a day! He won't have to worry about a thing."

She could also remember the sneer on her mother's face when the neighbor finally left.

"A *Shifter* for a son, can you imagine?" her mother had declared.

How mortified her parents would be now.

The sun had risen by the time Jessica made it past the factory district. Her parents would find out she was gone soon. She wondered if they would even look for her.

She was pulled back to the present by another muscle spasm, this one in her foot. It was like someone was trying to pull her toes out of their sockets. She stumbled and cried out in pain, flailing to grab something, anything, to break her fall. Her hands landed on a Shifter who was reading a sign that was posted on a nearby building. He squawked a protest as they fell into a heap on the sidewalk.

"*Eh*! What the—get off me!" the Shifter yelled, yanking himself free and standing back up. His hair was lank and greasy. His face was hard, no kindness to be seen behind his cold gray eyes. Several scars marred his face and neck, and one particularly large one ran right across his forehead, down through his eyebrow, and then continued below his eye on his cheek.

"S-sorry," Jessica panted as the pain dissipated. She struggled to her feet, her toes still throbbing.

The Shifter looked her up and down with a sneer. "You're far from home. You lost—or just stupid?"

"I-I, uh," Jessica stammered. She couldn't seem to form proper words.

The Shifter took a step toward her, and she took another step back. Her mind was racing, and she glanced around desperately for an escape route.

"Now you wouldn't be botherin' this young lady, would ya, Jack?" a deep voice behind Jessica drawled.

Jessica spun around and gasped.

The voice had come from the largest Shifter she'd ever seen. He towered over Jack and Jessica. She barely came to his elbow, yet something in his soft brown eyes made her feel... safe.

"Not at all, Ben," Jack said, his voice suddenly as oily as his hair. "This little lady and I were just getting acquainted."

The large Shifter whom Jack called Ben looked between Jack and Jessica.

"She don't look like she's really comfortable with gettin' to know you, Jack," Ben said. His voice was calm and even. "I think you should just git on your way."

Jack scowled, but as he was half Ben's size, he backed down. He shot Jessica a look right before he walked away that sent a shiver up her spine.

"You all right, ma'am?" Ben asked her once Jack was out of earshot.

Jessica nodded. "Thank you," she finally managed.

Now that Jack was gone, Ben smiled openly at Jessica. Something in his smile calmed her.

It was then Jessica realized that Ben didn't have the Shifter brand like the others.

Why is he here if he's not—? Her thought was interrupted when he spoke.

"I'm Ben," said Ben, falling in step with Jessica. "Where are you headed?"

"Jessica," Jessica replied. "I'm going to the airport."

"Well, ain't that a coinkydink!" Ben exclaimed. "I'm headed that way myself!"

Jessica found herself giggling at Ben's over-the-top elation. She soon found herself chatting along just as enthusiastically. *He must just be passing through...like me.*

"So why are you going to the airport, if you don't mind me askin'?" Ben asked.

Jessica hesitated. "My eighteenth birthday is today."

Ben nodded knowingly but said nothing.

"If I stay here, my parents will make me get the shifter test," Jessica continued. "And once they find out the results..." She trailed off.

"Where will you go?"

"Utopis. My boyfriend moved out there a couple months ago. I'm going to live with him."

"Won't that be the first place your parents look?"

Jessica shook her head. Bitterness creeping into her tone, she said, "They won't bother to look for me."

"I'm sure that's not true."

"Well, it is!" Jessica snapped.

Ben raised his eyebrows but didn't respond.

Jessica realized she was directing her fury at the wrong person. Again. They lapsed into an uneasy silence.

Several times Jessica opened her mouth to say something, but words failed her. Guilt wormed its way into her belly. Ben wasn't her parents. He didn't deserve her wrath.

"I'm sorry," she said, her voice cracking. "It's just...my parents..." She broke off. "It's complicated."

Ben smiled down at Jessica. "Don't worry about it."

They fell into step with each other, the silence a lot more comfortable now. Jessica was surprised when Ben spoke again.

"Well, I wish you all the best," Ben said, stopping suddenly.

Jessica looked up and realized they were standing at the airport entrance.

"Oh! Uh..." Jessica didn't know what to say.

Ben pulled out a tattered business card and handed it to her.

"If you find you need help, any at all, you can find me at this address," Ben said with a smile.

Jessica stuttered out a thank-you and looked down at the card. It was plain, just a white card with bold black letters that said "Shifter Outreach Program" and the address listed under it.

"Thank—" Jessica started to thank Ben again, but when she looked up he was already striding off down the street they'd just come from. Only as he disappeared down the block did it hit her: He'd never needed to come to the airport. He'd come for her. Just to make sure she made it safely.

Jessica looked down at the business card again and then shoved it into her bag. At least, she'd have *one* good memory about her birthday.

~*~

Jessica walked up to the front desk. A middle-aged woman sat typing on the computer, a look of eternal boredom etched on her face.

"Can I help you?" the woman monotoned as Jessica approached. She didn't look up from her computer.

"Hi, uh, I'd like to buy a ticket to Utopis?"

The woman typed for a few more seconds before answering. "I'll need to see your ID and your passport."

"Oh! Of course." Jessica dug around her bag for a moment, then produced the documents.

The woman finally looked up at Jessica as she took them from her. "Have you had your Shifter test done?"

Jessica opened her mouth, but no words came out. Her heart thudded against her ribs.

"Uh, no…no, I haven't."

"Sorry, ma'am, but the law now states that you must be able to produce a clean Shifter test before leaving the country."

"*What!?*"

Several sleepy travelers looked over at Jessica. She hadn't meant to shout, it had just sort of leapt out of her.

"I'm going to have to ask you not to shout at me, ma'am," the clerk said sharply.

"I'm sorry, I just…since when do you need a Shifter test to get on a plane?" Jessica tried to keep her voice light and cordial. Inside, she was becoming frantic. She'd planned this for *months*.

"New legislation came into effect this morning. No exceptions." The clerk handed Jessica back her ID and passport and turned back to the computer. "If you go get your test done today, you'll have your results in a couple hours, and they'll stamp your passport for you."

Jessica mumbled an insincere thank-you and stalked out of the airport. Frustration and fear piled on her until tears welled up in her eyes and threatened to spill over. She needed to do the Shifter test in order to leave the country, but once she did the test, she wouldn't be allowed to leave the country.

She sank down to the ground under a crooked tree, hidden by a fringe of untrimmed hedges. A stray branch caught her arm on the way down, leaving a long angry pink line in its wake. Her bag slumped down beside her. Her chest tightened, her breath coming too fast, too shallow. Her hands trembled as she wiped a stray tear from her cheek.

"I can't…" she whispered. "I can't do this. Wyatt—"

Pain lanced up her arm. A spasm—sharp and cruel. She screamed before she could stop herself. Tears came fast and hot, blurring the world as she sobbed. She curled into herself, wishing she could vanish.

Jessica's tears rolled off the bridge of her nose and into the dirt. Her plan—her whole future—had shattered. The world had closed its gates in her face, and she was stuck on the wrong side. Alone.

The Factory

Dear Diary,

Sarah didn't go to swimming yesterday. I tried texting her, but I didn't get an answer. Her dad answered when I called to check on her after practice.

"Sarah's gone," he practically growled into the phone. "Don't call here anymore." I heard what sounded like Sarah's mom wailing before he slammed the phone down.

I heard from Jason, whose younger brother is friends with Sarah's younger brother, that Sarah's Shifter test came back positive. That's why she wasn't at swimming yesterday. Our neighborhood is a gated community—Normals only.

I cried a little bit when I got home. Sarah and I have been in swimming together since we were toddlers. She was probably the person I was closest to, other than Jess. I knew she had her birthday over the weekend. I even knew she was going for her test. It never occurred to me that she—

She wanted to be a doctor. She even had an athletic scholarship. Now she won't ever get the chance.

The worst part is I have no way of contacting her anymore. Shifters aren't allowed cell phones. I don't even know if Shifters can even have home phones. I suppose if you don't have a home...

The atmosphere in the neighborhood is tense. It always is after...well, you know. Even Jess is subdued. We go through our lives thinking it couldn't possibly happen to us, to our friends. It only happens to the other guy, the less fortunate who don't have our impeccable bloodlines. Sarah is a reminder that it can happen to anyone, anywhere, no matter our status, our bloodlines.

I don't want to think about it anymore.

Love always,
Dani

~*~

Jessica stared up at the platform ladder, a heavy steel drill strapped to her back. She double checked the extension cord and her belt tools. Climbing all the way up to the top of the factory. only to forget something wasn't just annoying, it warranted punishment.

Her shoulders screamed by the halfway mark. The drill's strap bit into the brand on her neck, still pink and tender. She gritted her teeth. This was her fourth climb that morning, and it wasn't even break time.

This was her job—taking tools up to the workers on the platform and bringing down the tools they no longer needed. The platform supervisor often "accidentally" told her they were done with a tool, only to have her bring it back twenty minutes later. He was sadistic that way.

She hated it here. The work was mindless—load up, climb, unload, repeat. Each hour stretched like a rope pulled taut, and the tokens she earned each day didn't buy enough food. There were only two stores close by that would even accept the tokens. If she ever needed a new uniform or new shoes, she would have to go hungry for a few days to save up enough tokens to buy them.

~*~

She had tried to stay away from the factories. After the airport, she'd tried to scrape by on the streets.

The first night was rainy and cold—so cold. Jessica curled up under the awning of a shop, shivering, trying to escape the rain. The wind picked up shortly after midnight, blowing the rain sideways. In seconds, she was soaked to the bone. Defeated, she got up and hurried away.

A couple blocks down the street she ducked into an alley. Tarps were strung between the buildings. Several dishevelled Shifters huddled around two small metal barrels that blazed with small fires. Jessica hesitated at the edge of the tarps. An old Shifter smiled at her and beckoned her to join them.

Jessica didn't hesitate this time. Her teeth chattered as she approached the barrel. The Shifters parted, letting her get close to the heat. Another Shifter named Jane gave her a spare blanket. It was gray wool, itchy, and it smelled like wet dog.

"You won't last if you catch your death of cold out here, dear," Jane said firmly, wrapping the blanket around her shoulders.

Jane took Jessica under her wing. She introduced her to the other homeless Shifters, most of whom were seniors. Staying with them was safer than wandering around by herself. One of the anti-Shifter laws included a curfew. Those on their own after curfew tend to disappear.

Jane urged Jessica to go to one of the recruitment offices for the local factories.

"Most of us worked at the factories. It's good honest work. And you'll get to stay in the factory housing, better than shivering out here with the likes of us," Jane said.

"If you worked at the factories, why are you living out here?" Jessica asked.

"Once we got too old to do the work, we had to make room for the younger ones who took our place," Jane explained.

Jessica was outraged. "You mean you spent all those years working for these people, and once you weren't any use to them anymore, they threw you out on the street?!"

"That's just the way it is, dear."

"I'm not going to work in a factory," Jessica said defiantly. Her fists clenched. "I'm going to find a way out."

Jane smiled a sad, knowing smile. "I hope you do, dear."

Jessica reached the top, chest heaving. *So much for never ending up in a factory.*

~*~

Three days into her stint of homelessness, Jessica ran into someone she never expected to see again. Literally. They collided outside a storefront. Shopping bags fell, spilling their contents on the sidewalk.

"Oh, shit, I'm so sorry." Jessica dropped and fumbled to pick up the fallen shopping.

"Jess?!"

Jessica looked up and her face paled. She knew that face. Tiffany. Shit, what was her last name? She lived six houses down from her. Her father was a doctor at the Shifter Rehabilitation Center. She was a couple years older than Jessica.

"Uh, Tiff! Hey, what's up?" Jessica stammered, trying to smile like she wasn't wearing the same shirt for the third day in a row. She clamped her arms down to her sides. She smelled and she knew it.

Tiffany looked Jessica up and down. A flicker of disgust flashed on her face. "How are you? I haven't seen you for a few days! What are you doing here?" Tiffany tried and failed to hide her curiosity. Jessica knew just from her tone that gossip had already begun making its rounds through the neighborhood.

"I-I'm good, just looking for a..." Jessica's voice hitched, and she cleared her throat. "A good store for, um—"

"Oh, I know!" Tiffany squealed happily. "The Shifter stores have some of the cutest things! Like this one." Tiffany shook one of her newly packed shopping bags. "Tmhey have the cutest sweaters! And there's a shop down the street that has these really cute figurines! I'm trying to collect them all, but my allowance only covers one each month."

Jessica's head swam as Tiffany babbled about the bountiful shopping opportunities in the ghetto. She smiled politely and nodded every few minutes.

"And I got this purple one here. It's so cute!"

Pangs of envy at Tiffany's enthusiasm jabbed at Jessica. Was this really what she looked like just a few days ago? She couldn't even afford to eat, and here was this bitch complaining 'cause her allowance wasn't enough to finish her collection.

What she wouldn't give to be as carefree as Tiffany. To go back home and live her life with Wyatt without having to leave the safety of her neighborhood. Parts of her wanted to scream at Tiffany for daring to be Normal when she couldn't be.

A burst of bright laughter from down the street tugged at something in Jessica's memory. For a moment, Tiffany's voice blurred, and her mind spun backward to a winter evening—cold and beautiful, with Wyatt's crooked grin.

They were in his backyard tree house. It creaked when they shifted their weight, and the boards smelled like old leaves and sap. Jessica was snuggled up on his lap under a shared blanket she'd snuck out with.

"Your sister's birthday's in a couple weeks," he said, casually tossing a pebble through a knot in the wood. "Should we do something? Make her something?"

Jessica arched an eyebrow. "Like what? A scrapbook of all the times she yelled at us for sneaking out?"

Wyatt snorted, then looked up thoughtfully at Jessica. "What if we threw her a surprise party? We could get streamers and corny decorations from the dollar store. I might even be able to snitch a cake from that bakery over on Jefferson."

"She'd kill us," Jessica said, but her smile betrayed her.

"Nah, she loves us too much."

Jessica giggled and snuggled as close as their thick winter coats would let them.

Wyatt shifted, looking down at her. "We're gonna make it out of here someday, Jess. You and me. We're gonna do big things together."

Jessica remembered how safe that promise felt back then. How certain she'd been that he would keep it. She longed to go back to that moment under the blanket with Wyatt.

"I've got to go," Jessica cut in, sharper than she meant to. She didn't wait for Tiffany's reply, just turned and walked away.

She didn't look back. If she had, she might have laughed at the stunned look on Tiffany's face. She wasn't Normal. She never would be. But she wouldn't be a Shifter either. Not if she could help it.

~*~

Desperation brings out the worst in people.

The morning of the sixth day she woke up to find her bag raided. Everything valuable was gone—her money, her watch, the ring she had bought for Danielle, and a gold locket her grandparents had given her when she was five.

It was the ring that broke her. Silver with their birthstones set in a yin-yang design. An opal for her and a garnet for Danielle. She had worked doing odd jobs in her neighborhood for a year to save up for it.

Danielle was gone before she could give it to her.

Jane sat with her while she sobbed, murmuring comforting words. She lasted one day after the robbery. Just one.

Her stomach twisted with cramps. Her hands shook. She felt lightheaded. Eighteen years of steady meals hadn't prepared her for real hunger.

By the next morning, she couldn't take it anymore.

She walked herself to the nearest factory recruitment center. By nightfall, she was tested and branded, just another number in the system. She'd traded her freedom for food and shelter. She did what she had to do to survive.

That didn't stop the shame.

~*~

Jessica was panting by the time she made it to the top of the ladder. Her arms shook as she unloaded the heavy drill and extension cord. She resisted the urge to scratch the pink- tinged scab where her brand was. It had gotten infected. Normal, her coworkers said. Expected even. The more Shifters who die of infection, the better. Less mouths to feed.

The platform supervisor stalked over, smirking.

"What the hell is that?" he sneered.

Jessica ground her teeth. Her hands tightened around the extension cord.

"You asked for the drill," she said through gritted teeth.

"No, I specifically asked for two grinders. And make sure you bring batteries with them this time. Take this thing back down, it's just in the way up here."

Jessica muttered every swear word she knew under her breath as she repacked the drill and cord and started back down the ladder.

It took Jessica nearly half an hour to find everything—grinders, batteries, and any other damn accessory they might need. When she finally ascended to the platform again, the supervisor was waiting for her with another Shifter named George. Jessica's stomach clenched. His main job on the platform was drilling holes in the steel beams.

"Where's the drill?" George asked, exasperated. "I thought you were supposed to bring it up like forty-five minutes ago."

Jessica glared at the supervisor, who was standing behind George with that vicious grin on his stupid face.

"I did bring it up, but *he* told me to take it back down and bring these instead." Jessica showed George the grinders strapped to her belt.

George looked quizzically back at the supervisor, who feigned an innocent look. He turned back to Jessica and nodded with a sigh. The expression on his face said it all—he'd seen this shit before, and he was done with it.

"I don't know what she's talking about. I clearly told her to bring up the drill for you. Either she doesn't listen very well or she's too stupid to—"

The grinder slammed into his face with a sickening crack!

He crumpled.

Jessica panted, red-faced with anger. She was holding the other grinder in her hand. She didn't remember taking them off her belt.

For a moment, neither she nor George moved.

"What do you think you're *doing?*" George hissed at her. He pulled the remaining grinder out of her still-shaking hand and glanced around. The other workers didn't seem to be aware of what had happened yet.

Color slowly drained from Jessica's face as panic welled up in her gut. Her chest tightened, and she stared wide-eyed at George.

What the hell did I just do?!

"What—what do I do?" she whispered desperately.

"Go," he said, low and sharp. Another worker was heading their way. "Pack your things and get out of the city as fast as you can."

Jessica didn't wait to be told twice. She was down the ladder in record time. She only stopped long enough to shed the heavy toolbelt before bolting for the door.

~*~

Jessica slammed through the apartment door, her lungs burning. She didn't stop running until her knees hit the floor inside. George gave her a chance to get away, and she wouldn't waste it. She wasn't foolish enough to think he would cover for her. Even letting her go was enough to warrant punishment. He might be paying for it already.

She tore open her old book bag, heart racing.

What do I need? Where can I go? Think. THINK!

Her hands fumbled—clothes, food packets, rolled socks. The bag slipped. Its contents spilled out on the floor.

"Shit!" Dropping to her knees, she fumbled to gather everything up. Amid the clutter, something white caught her eye.

A card.

She stared at it for a moment. *Shifter Outreach Program.* The words took a few extra seconds to register. Then she remembered.

"If you ever need help…" Ben's voice echoed, faint, nearly forgotten from that first miserable day.

Jessica ran her finger over the raised letters. *Shifter Outreach Program.* Would they still help her after what she'd done?

Jessica memorized the address and shoved the card into her pocket.

There was only one way to find out.

Flight and Pancakes

Dear Diary,

I'm going to college!

I got the letter in the mail today. I've been accepted into the Institute for Science and Technology over in Grand Chet! Pending my clean Shifter test, of course. Most colleges won't allow Shifters to attend. I wonder if they know how much potential they are wasting, keeping Shifters from higher education. It's not fair. I said this one night at dinner, and Mom and Dad practically shouted themselves hoarse telling me how wrong I am. Shifters have no place in civil society, they said, they're no better than the animals they turn into.

Shifters are constantly protesting how unfair everything is, but nothing ever changes. They just keep coming out with more restrictions. When I find the cure, all will be put right. Shifters will be allowed to go everywhere we are.

Jessi snuck out again last night. She climbs out the window onto the porch roof and climbs down the oak tree. I don't know how she manages it. The gap between the tree and the porch roof is huge! I swear the girl has no fear.

We had new neighbors moved in three months ago, and Jessi is absolutely puppy-dog in love with their son, Wyatt. He is the same age as Jessi, and he seems like a nice kid. I confronted Jessi when she snuck back in last night, and she swears up and down that they didn't do anything other than talk. I'm skeptical, but Jessi has never been one to lie to me, so I will give her the benefit of the doubt and not tell Daddy. I did give her a stern talking to about being smart and not letting boys talk her into things that she's not ready for. She made a face and rolled her eyes at me.

"I'm not stupid, Dani." Boy, this kid has gotten sassy! She is really smart though. I'm glad. I won't have to worry about her when I leave.

Only eight more months until my eighteenth birthday, and then I'm college bound!

Love always,
Dani

~*~

Jessica walked quickly, her head down. Her factory uniform made her feel exposed—like a walking target. Her old clothes had been tossed in a bin marked "Donations" when she got her factory uniforms.

Jessica lifted her head briefly to see where she was. Having the address was one thing, but she'd never been to this part of town before. None of the street names matched the address, and none of them looked familiar. She didn't dare ask for directions until she got further from the factory.

Police sirens wailed nearby. Jessica flinched so hard her shoulder hit a store's mailbox. She ducked into the store and pretended to browse a rack of T-shirts.

A police car screamed by the store. Another followed close behind.

A hand on her shoulder made Jessica jump and shriek.

"I'm so sorry, dear, I didn't mean to scare you—Oh my, you're white as a ghost! Come along, dear, come sit in the back and collect yourself."

Jessica protested weakly as she was ushered away by surprisingly strong wrinkled hands. The hands belonged to an older woman with curly white hair wearing a flower print shirt that had an employee tag labeled "Maggie" pinned to it.

Maggie took Jessica through a small hallway and up a flight of stairs at the back of the store. The stairs opened up into a kitchen, small but clean and bright.

"Sit down right here, dear. What did you say your name was?" Maggie pulled a chair out from under the little kitchen table under the window.

"Uh, Jessica," Jessica said hesitantly.

She sat, and not a moment later, Maggie placed a mug of coffee in front of her. Then a bowl of sugar and what looked like powdered milk.

"There, you drink up. I'll be right back. I just need to tell my husband to watch the store."

"Thank you." Jessica's voice shook.

Maggie patted her shoulder in a tender way that reminded Jessica of her grandmother.

Jessica spooned some sugar and powdered milk into her coffee and stirred. The warm coffee burned against her frozen hands. She took a sip, savoring the warmth as it filled her. Then she made a face and added two more spoonfuls of sugar.

Maggie came back into the kitchen followed by a large elderly man. He was close to six feet tall and bald headed, with a large round belly. His face bore the lines of a man well past his prime, but his eyes twinkled with mischief. Jessica noted that neither Maggie nor her husband had Shifter brands.

"Maggie said we had a stray in the kitchen," the man boomed. "What do you think you're doing here?"

Jessica's eyes widened. "I, uh, I mean, uh—"

"Oh, for Christ's sake, Marvin, get outta here. You're scaring her." Maggie swatted at him with an oven mitt.

He chuckled and left, but not before he gave Jessica a cheeky grin and a wink. His heavy footsteps receded down the stairs.

Maggie pulled out a mixing bowl and placed it on the counter. "Are you hungry, dear?"

"Oh, uh, I'm good, thank you."

She may as well have been talking to the wall. Maggie was already scooping flour into the bowl. A few minutes later, Jessica was listening to the sizzle of pancake batter in a pan.

The smell of pancakes filled the kitchen—sweet, warm, unreal. Jessica's mouth watered, but her heart twisted.

Don't trust her. Don't trust anyone.

While the pancakes sizzled in the pan, Jessica let herself be swept back to her mother's kitchen—back to a time when her mother still made pancakes for her. Before Dani was ripped from their lives.

She remembered bursting through the back door, tears streaming down her face.

"Sweetheart, what's the matter?" her mother asked her, rushing forward.

"They...she..." Jessica was crying too hard to speak.

Her mom pulled her into a hug and held her until her sobs softened into hiccups.

"All right, here, now sit here and tell me. What happened that has you all upset?"

Jessica's face crumpled in anguish as she sat down with her mom.

"C-Claire told me that Becky t-told her that Toby likes me." She whimpered between sniffles. "Th-they convinced me to write a n-note to him and—oh, Mom." A fresh wave of tears spilled down her cheeks.

"What happened? Did he not really like you?" her mom murmured, stroking her hair.

"He read th-the note out to the whole c-class when the teacher went to the bathroom!" Jessica wailed.

"Oh, honey," her mom soothed, pulling her back into a hug.

Jessica sobbed into her mother's shoulder until she had nothing left.

"Why would they do that to me?" she whispered, blotchy and exhausted.

"I don't know, baby," her mother said, handing her a tissue. "It just goes to show you can't trust everyone. Not even your friends."

The clatter of plates brought Jessica back to the present. Maggie set a plate of pancakes in front of her, along with a bottle of syrup. After a few moments of hesitation, Jessica ate ravenously. Better pancakes never had nor never would be had again.

Maggie refilled her plate each time it emptied. Finally, Jessica pushed the plate away and told Maggie no more, claiming she was "full to the brim."

"How are you feeling, dear? Better?" Maggie asked, sitting down at the table with her own mug of coffee.

"I…" Jessica hesitated. The logical part of her brain was screaming at her to not trust this stranger. Especially since neither she nor her husband had Shifter brands. The scared little girl in her heart, however, was desperate for someone to care. Jessica met Maggie's gaze, her soft brown eyes both friendly and genuinely concerned.

Jessica burst into tears. Her defenses crumbled. Between sobs, she told Maggie everything. Not just about the factory incident, but about Danielle's disappearance, her failed plan with Wyatt, her family—everything.

Maggie stood and pulled Jessica into an embrace. Jessica sobbed on the old woman's shoulder.

"There, there, it's all right, dear," Maggie soothed. "Sometimes things don't go our way, but that doesn't mean we give up. We just have to find another way."

Jessica clung to her until her sobs gave way to little hiccups.

"Wha—*hic*—what do I do?"

"You just don't worry about that right now. Right now we'll just worry about getting you some clean clothes. Tonight after the store is closed, my husband and I will get in touch with the people who can help you."

A fresh wave of tears washed over Jessica. She thanked Maggie over and over again between sobs.

"Don't thank me yet, dear," Maggie said, voice low. "We're nowhere near safe."

Jessica wiped her eyes and nodded. She wasn't safe—but she wasn't alone anymore either.

~*~

Jessica stood in the doorway to her parent's dining room. She could smell her mother's pot roast, hear her father asking Dani when her next swim meet was. It felt so real. She reached out to her sister.

"Wait, Dani…," she tried to call, but no sound came out.

Pain shot through her arms and legs. Her joints shifted and cracked like dry branches. She fell forward, screaming—

And landed with a thump on Maggie's living-room carpet.

Maggie peeked through the door to the kitchen. "You okay, dear?"

"Yeah." Jessica groaned and pulled herself up. She checked her limbs gingerly, wincing as she bent her knees and elbows. Her joints ached like she'd run a marathon in her sleep.

Maggie handed Jessica a white pill and a glass of water when she entered the kitchen.

"What—?"

"Aspirin," answered Maggie before Jessica could finish her question. "Trust me, it'll help."

The source of the pot roast smell in Jessica's dream revealed itself with the loud beep of a timer. Maggie pulled a roasting pan out of the oven, and Jessica's mouth started watering. In moments, Maggie had the roast on a plate next to bowls of potatoes, corn, carrots and peas, and gravy.

Just then the stairs creaked and groaned with the approach of heavy footsteps. The kitchen door swung open, and Marvin walked in carrying a little girl who couldn't be older than five. He was followed by a young woman who was carrying another little girl, clearly the first one's younger sister.

"Gramma!" the two girls squealed in unison and squirmed to the floor.

Maggie knelt down, beaming, and embraced them.

"Oh, you girls are getting so big!" Maggie exclaimed. She gave each girl a kiss, and they ran into the living room, giggling.

"You two stay out of Gramma and Grampa's room!" the young woman called after them as she shrugged off her coat.

Collective groans came from the living room, and the adults chuckled.

Jessica took this chance to take a quick glance at the young woman. Her curly hair was pulled back in a ponytail and gold hoop earrings hung from her earlobes. She was around Jessica's height, but next to Marvin she looked tiny. A small but clearly defined baby bump showed under her shirt.

"Hey, Maggie," the young woman said. "How are you?"

"I'm just fine, Ellie, darling."

Jessica tried to retreat discreetly into the corner of the room. She felt like an intruder in the middle of a private family moment.

"What are you still doin' here?" Marvin boomed, making Jessica jump.

"I, uh, I—" Jessica stuttered. She was so flustered she didn't catch the mischievous glint in Marvin's eye or the grin on his face.

"Will you stop scarin' that poor girl!" Maggie exclaimed, exasperated. "Jessica, this is my daughter-in-law, Ellie."

"Right." Ellie nodded and Jessica thought she saw her and Maggie exchange furtive looks. "Nice to meet you, Jessica."

Jessica stumbled over her words for a moment, still rattled by Marvin's loud exclamation. "Uh, you too."

Maggie pulled a stack of plates out of the cupboard and set them down on the small kitchen table.

"Help yourself, Jessica dear," she said with a smile.

Marvin was in the middle of slicing the pot roast when more footsteps pounded up the stairs.

"Sorry, I'm late!" a familiar voice burst through the door.

Jessica almost dropped her plate. Standing at the door shedding his coat was none other than Ben! Her mouth dropped open, too stunned to speak for a moment.

"I know you!" she blurted out finally.

Ben grinned down at her. "Good to see ya again! From the airport, right? How ya doin'?"

Jessica was too shocked and confused to form a coherent answer. Luckily, Ben didn't wait for one. He grabbed a plate and started filling it with food, chatting with Marvin and being fussed over by Maggie.

Once their plates were filled, Maggie and Marvin took their food into the living room with the children, leaving Jessica at the small kitchen table with Ben and Ellie.

"So," Ben said casually between forkfuls, "tell me everything."

Jessica retold her story to Ben and Ellie. Tears threatened to fall as she spoke, but she blinked them away stubbornly.

"Then I ducked into the store, and Maggie brought me up here," Jessica finished.

"So what do you want to do?" Ellie asked gently.

"I…" Jessica's voice cracked. What did she want?

She wanted Danielle. She wanted to wake up in her own bed and hear her parents chatting over breakfast. She wanted Danielle to come into her room and yell at her for reading her diary again. She wanted…

"Wyatt," she whispered. "I want to get out of here, go to Utopis, and find Wyatt."

Ben and Ellie exchanged looks. "That won't be easy," Ben said at last. "There are a lot of miles between here and the border, and there are more guards out every day."

"Then what do I *do*?" Jessica asked desperately.

"You come with us. We'll do everything we can to get you where you want to be," Ellie said, placing her hand on Jessica's. Her small hand was warm, steady.

"That's right, we'll do our very best," Ben boomed enthusiastically.

For the first time that day, Jessica felt almost calm. She didn't know if she trusted them—not yet. But it was more than she'd had that morning, and maybe—maybe that was enough.

Run-In with a Bear

Dear Diary,

It's only been three weeks since I got my acceptance letter, but it feels like it's been a year. I swear time couldn't go slower if it tried. Why can't it be my birthday already!

School ended a week ago, and Jess has been gone every single day. I've seen her all over the neighborhood cutting grass, weeding gardens, trimming trees. Mom says she's saving up so she can elope with that neighbor boy, Wyatt. She's kidding, I think. Jess is only fourteen! Still, she is with him an awful lot. I don't think they've gone more than a weekend without seeing each other, and that's only because we went up to Auntie Melanie's for Candace's birthday last month. Auntie Melanie, Uncle Frank, and Candace live over in West Selhen, which is four hours away.

I'm not a big fan of Candace. She and I are only eight months apart age-wise, but she acts like she's so much better than me just because she lives in a Shifter-free town. West Selhen doesn't have a Shifter ghetto like our town does. She and I got in an argument while we were there 'cause she said none of us should have to share living space with any of them. *She spat out the word* "them" *like it was something rotten. I reminded her that the only reason she could afford to live in this big, fancy house is because of* them. *Uncle Frank owns one of the factories that is run by Shifters over in Fort Nagreen. She just gave me one of her superior looks and told me I would understand when I grow up. As if she's sooo much older than me!*

I'm getting angry again just writing this down. I'm going to take a break and calm down. Maybe see if Jess wants to go to the movies tonight. That new one with Ashina is out now.

Love Always,
Dani

~*~

Jessica shifted, then swore. A splinter jabbed deep into her upper arm, and it *hurt*. She closed her eyes, gritted her teeth, and tried to focus on her breathing.

A knot had formed in her stomach the moment Ben led her down to the car and popped the trunk. He lifted the carpet to reveal a long wooden box that had been built into the car where the spare tire should have been. It looked too much like a coffin, a shallow splinter-ridden tomb.

"I can't fit in there!" she exclaimed, taking a step back.

"It's the only way," said Ben patiently. "We have to go back through a security checkpoint, and we have no ID for you yet."

"What if they check the trunk? What if I run out of air before we get there and you have a dead body in the trunk and they find it, won't that be worse?" Jessica was rambling, and she knew it, but she couldn't seem to stop.

Ben sat down so he was eye level with Jessica. "Hey…look at me." He waited patiently for her to look at him. "Take a deep breath. Good. I promise you will get there safe. This isn't the first time we've done this, y'know. You will not suffocate. There are air holes." Ben placed a huge hand on her shoulder, nearly knocking her down.

Jessica scowled at him. His simple, calm logic irked her.

But he was right, and she knew it.

So she lay in the secret compartment focusing on breathing and ignoring the throbbing in her arm. The mingling smell of oil and sawdust made her stomach turn. Every bump shoved the rogue sliver deeper into her skin.

It was simple, Ben had explained. He would take Ellie and the girls home, then smuggle Jessica to a safe place. Easy-peasy.

A few minutes into the drive, the car slowed to a stop. A new voice from the front of the car made Jessica freeze. They were at the checkpoint. She was suddenly aware of how loud she was breathing. Surely, the guard could hear her and would order them to open the trunk. She instinctively pressed herself further into the wood, as if that would somehow make her invisible.

"Where are you coming from, and where are you headed?"

The guard's no-nonsense voice was muffled; Jessica could just barely hear him.

"We were at my in-laws for dinner, and now we're heading home," Ellie's steady voice betrayed nothing.

"Can I see your identification, please?"

There was a short silence. She imagined Ellie pulling her ID out of her purse.

"How about you, sir? Can I see your identification, please?"

"Of course," Ben's good-natured voice replied.

Another silence. Any minute now they were going to order them to open the trunk. Jessica had heard stories about the checkpoints that went out of the ghetto. Shifters were often detained and searched, even thrown in jail for trying to smuggle things. Fake IDs were another big issue, Shifters trying to pass themselves off as Normals. Jessica barely dared to breathe.

"Have a good night, ma'am."

Jessica's head spun as the car pulled forward.

They *made* it.

~*~

Jessica forced herself to take calming breaths. She never would have thought herself claustrophobic before, but she definitely did now.

Just remember, you're doing this for Wyatt.

She clung to her memory of him to keep her sane. She let her mind wander, let herself slip back to the first time they'd met. The day she fell hopelessly in love with him.

She was fourteen at the time. She and Courtney M (not to be mixed up with Courtney L, who was a raging bitch if ever there was one) were just leaving Jessica's house. They had just gotten permission from

Jessica's parents to go to the library, so naturally they headed to the mall. As they passed the house next to Jessica's, the front door swung open, and *he* stepped out.

He was everything Jessica had ever dreamed of. His sandy-brown hair was styled in an effortlessly messy way. He wore a plain black jacket over a white T-shirt and blue jeans along with beat up high tops. A lopsided grin lit up his face, the most beautiful face in the history of faces.

"Hey," he said as he approached, his grin growing wider as his green eyes flicked between Jessica and her friend. Or were they hazel?

Jessica forgot how to breathe.

He stopped a few feet away, hands shoved in his jacket pockets. "So you guys live around here?"

Jessica opened her mouth, but no sound came out. She forgot how to form words. Courtney M elbowed her in the ribs.

"I, uh, right there." Jessica jerked her thumb at her house, cursing herself inwardly for sounding like a complete idiot.

"I live around the corner," Courtney M said, flashing a flirty smile at him.

"Cool," he said. His eyes rested on Jessica for a moment, and her heart flip-flopped in her chest. "Maybe I'll, uh, see you 'round?"

"Yeah, sure," Courtney M said. "I'm Courtney, by the way."

"Wyatt," Wyatt said. He looked expectantly at Jessica, who blinked like an idiot until Courtney M gave her another elbow to the ribs.

"Jessica," she croaked.

"Cool. Well, see ya, Courtney. Jessica." Wyatt winked at Jessica, then turned and strolled off.

"Hello? Earth to Jess," Courtney M waved a hand in front of Jessica's face as soon as Wyatt was out of earshot.

"I think I'm in love," Jessica sighed.

~*~

An eternity later, the trunk creaked open. Blinding light flooded in, and Ben's face appeared—calm and smiling.

"Oh, thank *god*," Jessica groaned.

Ben laughed and helped Jessica out of the trunk.

They were in a forest. Jessica had never seen one. Not in person. Her knees wobbled as she stepped into the cathedral of trees. The stories hadn't done them justice. Towering trunks loomed all around her. A light breeze played through the boughs, shushing the city and its constant noise. Branches creaked and groaned against each other. Jessica's breath caught in her throat. Under the canopy, even with the leaves gone in the autumn winds, the darkness was complete.

"This way," Ben whispered. He grabbed Jessica's hand and led her into the forest.

They trekked through the forest. Ben's massive body made a path through the underbrush, and Jessica followed close behind. Branches grabbed at her sleeves and hair, sometimes breaking off with no resistance, sometimes yanking hard and holding her back. More than once Ben had to come back and rescue her.

Distance blurred. All Jessica knew was the fire in her legs. Autumn rains had transformed the forest floor into a mud pit that sucked Jessica's feet down with every step. Cold muddy water sloshed into her shoes, soaking her feet. More than once Ben had to pull her out of the mud.

Finally, when Jessica was sure she couldn't make it one more step, Ben stepped out of the brush and onto a path. Jessica scrambled up onto the solid ground and collapsed. The cold night air burned as it entered her lungs, and she coughed uncontrollably.

"C'mon, we can't stop yet," urged Ben, reaching down to help her up. "We're nearly there, I promise."

Jessica's limbs trembled under her own weight as she stood. She stumbled so wildly Ben had to catch her to keep her from falling. Her legs shook violently, and her feet were numb.

"I c-can't feel my-my feet." Jessica's teeth chattered so hard she could barely speak.

"C'mere." Ben turned and crouched down.

Jessica wrapped her arms around his neck, and he stood up like she weighed nothing. He ran up the path faster than Jessica expected from someone his size.

All of a sudden Ben stopped in his tracks. Jessica couldn't see past his bulk, but a cold voice cut through the silence of the forest.

"Get down on the ground! Keep your hands where we can see them!"

Ben slowly got to his knees and lowered Jessica to the ground. Two men dressed in the black police uniforms pointed guns at them.

"You!" The closer guard pointed his gun at Ben. "You have no cause to be out here! This is a restricted area! Explain yourself!"

Jessica's heart sank to her frozen feet. There was no way Ben could talk his way out of this. They were done. She was going to get taken away and—

Coarse brown fur hit Jessica in the face, and something large knocked her over. In the light of the guards' flashlights, a huge brown bear towered over them where Ben had just stood. With one swipe of its massive paw, it knocked the guns out of the guards' hands.

The bear moved fast. One swipe. Two swipes. Guns clattered to the ground. Screaming, so much screaming. A wet crunch that she later realized was multiple bones breaking.

Jessica sat in the mud just off the path. She heard the screams, but she couldn't move, couldn't breathe. She couldn't seem to process what she was witnessing.

The screaming stopped with one last sickening *snap*.

The bear turned to face her. Blood stained its muzzle. Jessica scrambled to her feet and backed up a step. She backed up slowly until her back hit the rough bark of a tree. The bear sat back on his haunches, waiting patiently. She glanced over at the motionless outlines of the guards. One of their flashlights illuminated the bodies. Bile rose in Jessica's throat. She turned and fell to her hands and knees. The beautiful roast dinner Maggie had worked so hard on landed at the base of the tree.

Jessica retched again, heaving until she had nothing left. When she was done, she sat back on her heels. She wiped her mouth on the back of her sleeve.

"Hey."

Ben's voice startled Jessica. She whipped around and scrambled back around the tree so it was between her and him.

"Whoa, it's okay, I'm not going to hurt you," said Ben quietly.

So many thoughts raced through Jessica's mind she couldn't speak for a moment. Her chest tightened. Too tight. She couldn't breathe.

A bear. He changed—into a bear. He *killed* them.

Her heart slammed against her ribs like it was trying to escape. Her breaths came in short, sharp gasps. She couldn't breathe, couldn't think.

"Hey, come on now. You gotta calm down." Ben took a step toward Jessica.

She clambered back.

"You…you," she stammered, trying—and failing—to form a coherent sentence. "You're a *Shifter*!"

Ben raised an eyebrow. "Yes, I am," he stated simply.

"Well…but…I…" Jessica sputtered. Her thoughts were scattered. Then she noticed. "You're naked!" she blurted out. She turned her head, her face burning.

Ben chuckled. "Well, you couldn't expect my clothes to fit on an eight-hundred-pound grizzly, could you?"

Jessica grunted, not turning her head.

"Look, we can't stop, not yet. We still have a ways to go." Ben held out a hand to Jessica.

She eyed it suspiciously.

"I promised I'd get you there safe, remember?"

Jessica looked warily at his hand, at the blood drying on his face. She peeked over at the corpses.

He'd brought her this far. *But he was one of them.* He'd saved her. *But he was one of them.*

She closed her eyes, just for a second, then she reached out and took Ben's hand.

What else could she do?

The Owl and the Ocean

Dear Diary,

It's like 2:00 a.m. right now, but I can't sleep so I may as well write to you. I woke up with a nasty charley horse in my leg, and it still hurts.

These past couple weeks have been crazy! I've woken up almost every night with a charley horse, and I am absolutely exhausted. I think it's from all the extra practice I've been doing. I had a swim meet on Saturday, and I got second place overall! I got first in butterfly and freestyle, but second in backstroke, and third in breaststroke. They also give points for form which helped. There was only two-point difference between me and the girl who got first.

I think I must have caught something at the pool though, because I spent the last two days stuck in bed. I had a cough and a stuffy nose and a nasty headache. It was the worst. I thought my head was going to explode. I had to get Daddy to tape my curtains shut and keep a cool cloth over my eyes. Mom wanted to take me to a doctor, but I told her it was just the sinus pressure from the stuffy nose.

Jess and Wyatt are dating. They think no one else knows, but they are super bad at hiding it. Always holding hands and staring at each other adoringly when they think no one else is looking. I tried talking to Jess again, to make sure she's being careful. She just scoffed and told me to mind my own business. I'll admit, I snapped at her a bit. I got mad and told her it was my business because she's my sister and I don't want to become an aunt before I go to college. She got all red in the face and yelled that I'm not her mother and she's not a moron and she's not going to do that until she's good and ready and even when she is ready it still won't be my business. She stomped out and slammed the door and didn't come back until after curfew. She got grounded for that and didn't speak to me for three whole days.

The aching in my leg is finally dying down. I think I'm gonna try and go back to sleep.

Love Always,
Dani

~*~

Jessica's feet throbbed with each step she took. Ben, who had tied his tattered T-shirt around his waist as a makeshift covering, was leading her further and further into the woods. She almost asked, again, if they were there yet, then thought better of it. Probably best not to annoy the person who can turn into a bear.

Still she needed to do something to distract herself from her throbbing feet. So she asked the question that had been buzzing around the back of her mind.

"How"—she swallowed the lump in her throat—"how do you not have a brand?"

Ben smiled that good-natured smile of his. "Easy. I never got tested, not officially anyway."

"But how?" Jessica had never heard of a Shifter *not* getting tested before. They had to be tested to go to college, get their driver's license, get a job…It was unheard of. Especially in her neighborhood.

"I was lucky. My parents were both raised by Shifters. They saw how hard it was for their parents, and they promised each other they wouldn't put their kids through that."

"Oh," was all Jessica could say. She tried to swallow the lump that formed in her throat when she thought of her own parents. They would never have allowed her to go without getting tested. Their status in the neighborhood was too important. If she closed her eyes, she could see the looks on their faces the day Danielle got tested. She didn't know which was worse, Dad's red-faced anger or Mom's haunted grief.

Just when she thought she couldn't go a step further, Ben stopped in front of her. Just ahead of them, in a small clearing, stood a small whitewashed building. It reminded Jessica of the old one-room schoolhouses she'd seen in her history books. Or maybe an old church.

"I'm going to make sure the coast is clear," Ben whispered. "You stay here." He crept forward silently.

Jessica couldn't help but wonder how someone so big could be so stealthy. Just as Ben disappeared into the darkness ahead, a sound Jessica had never heard before sounded from somewhere in the forest. She jumped, her heart pounding in her chest. She peered into the darkness around her, but couldn't see anything.

"*Reeeeeee!*"

The sound was louder this time. Jessica's heart jumped to her throat. Did Ben lead her out here to get eaten?

A shape swooped down from the canopy with a loud *reeeee*! Jessica shrieked and ducked. She looked up wildly, but the shape was nowhere to be seen.

Ben appeared from the gloom. "You all right?"

"I…something, something attacked me!" Jessica exclaimed, still looking around wildly.

"*Reeeeeeeee!*"

The sound came from directly above their heads. Jessica jumped out of her skin. The red flush of embarrassment crept up her face as Ben tried—and failed—to stifle his laughter.

"What's so funny?" she demanded.

"That's…that's nothin' but a…a bitty little owl," Ben gasped. "I'm sorry, I…I shouldn't laugh but…you should-a seen your face."

Jessica scowled. Ben only laughed harder.

Finally, when Ben regained his composure, he waved a hand for Jessica to follow him. He led her up to the building and opened the door slowly.

A loud creak announced their presence. A narrow hall led into a large open room with a pulpit at the front. Wooden pews were shoved haphazardly against one wall. Every step they took echoed through the empty space.

"C'mon," Ben urged.

Jessica followed him behind the pulpit.

Just as Ben bent down behind the pulpit, a screech at the window made Jessica jump once again. She and Ben wheeled around to see a small shadow sitting on the ledge of one of the broken windows. It hopped into the room and fluttered down to the floor near them.

It was a bird. At least, it looked like one. It was bigger than the birds she'd seen around her neighborhood. A ring of brown feathers around its snowy white face was heart-shaped, and it had a sharp, narrow beak that curved down at the end. Inch-long claws clicked on the wood floor as it hopped toward them.

Danielle had loved the birds. She'd gotten in so much trouble when her mother caught her feeding—

Jessica froze. It was growing. Its limbs lengthened. Feathers disappeared. Bones shifted with audible creaks and crunches. The next minute, a girl stood where the bird had been, barefoot and smiling.

"Hey," she said, shaking out brown hair that matched the bird's brown feathers. A single tiny braid adorned one side of her head. Stuck in the end of the braid was a white and brown feather with four brown splotches along the shaft. Ben's flashlight shone on her neck illuminating the brand in sharp relief. She stuck out a hand to Jessica.

"I'm Cassandra. You can call me Cassie."

"I…Jessica," said Jessica, shaking her hand.

Her hands were thin, but strong, and her nails were long and rounded almost to a point. Jessica then realized that Cassie was also naked. She blushed and looked away. This was definitely something she wouldn't get used to any time soon.

"Looks like you two ran into a bit of trouble," Cassie said, looking down at Ben. He'd wiped most of the blood off on his tattered clothes, but there was still some streaked on his arms and face.

"Just a couple nosy guards down the road," Ben grunted.

"One day one of those *nosy guards* is gonna get the better of you," Cassie warned.

"It'll take more than a couple nosy guards to take me down," Ben grunted again and stood up.

Jessica watched in amazement as he picked the entire pulpit up along with a piece of the floor. It swung up, suspended by metal poles that locked in place with another click. Under it, a dark hole opened. Jessica shivered.

"All right, get in, quick," Ben urged quietly.

Cassie sat and lowered herself into the hole. Jessica approached hesitantly. She looked up at Ben, who smiled down at her encouragingly.

"It's not that far down, I promise," he whispered.

Jessica gave him a tight smile and sat down at the edge of the hole. Slowly, she lowered herself down, and taking a deep breath, she let go.

Ben was right; it wasn't that far down. A flashlight came on in the tunnel just as Jessica's feet hit the ground. She looked around, blinking stupidly, trying to adjust to the sudden light. Cassie was just pulling a bright-yellow polka-dotted sundress over her head.

"You two okay down there?" Ben's voice floated down the hole.

"Yeah, we're good," Cassie called back.

"All righty then, I'm gonna head back before the patrols find my car."

"You're not coming?" Jessica blurted.

Ben chuckled low. "Sorry. Jess, I hafta get back to Ellie and the girls. 'Sides, I can't fit down that teeny hole." His voice changed slightly from lighthearted to comforting. "Cass'll take good care of you, I promise."

"Don't worry, I won't bite," Cassie joked, giving Jessica a reassuring smile.

Jessica tried to smile back, but it turned into a sort of grimace.

"I'll check in later this week," Ben promised. He unlocked the pulpit and set it back in place with a gentle thud. Muffled footsteps headed in the direction of the door, and then… silence.

Jessica stared up at the empty space above her. She felt almost— alone—without Ben.

~*~

"You ready?" Cassie asked gently. Her smile was patient, encouraging.

Jessica took a deep breath and pushed down the knot of anxiety in her gut.

"Yeah. Let's go."

Jessica followed Cassie through the tunnel. They passed several other tunnels that branched off in different directions. Cassie stayed silent, seeming to sense Jessica's need for it. She didn't want to talk anymore tonight.

Her legs were beginning to tremble with fatigue when a strange noise reached her ears. Low wooshes and the odd splash of water. A few steps later a cool breeze brushed her cheek. Slowly, the darkness of the tunnel gave way to a silver-blue light.

Jessica stopped in her tracks. The sight before her stole her breath. The mouth of the tunnel opened to a sandy beach. She'd only ever seen a beach in pictures before. They didn't prepare her for reality. Moonlight danced across endless water that never seemed to stop moving. Silver ripples chased each other to the shore.

Jessica stared, wide-eyed. A breeze ruffled her hair, bringing with it a new scent—a sharp, salty, wet smell.

"The ocean," Cassie answered the question Jessica couldn't form.

Dani's face swam through her memory unbidden. She had been obsessed with seeing the ocean someday. She'd talked of nothing else for months when she was thirteen, and as far as Jessica knew, she'd never given up the dream.

Jessica's stomach tightened. It should be Dani here, taking in the beauty and power in front of her. Not her.

Cassie steered Jessica up the beach and into a forest, Jessica struggling on the loose sand. By the time they reached the forest, she was breathing hard.

After a brief rest at the edge of the forest to catch her breath, Jessica forced her exhausted legs to stumble behind Cassie. Not long after entering the forest, a huge seemingly abandoned warehouse loomed into view.

"That's where we're going," Cassie whispered. "It's a safe house for people like us."

Cassie didn't head toward the boarded-up doors, or even the cracked black windows. Instead, she led Jessica to an ancient cellar door in the ground, much like the storm cellars in her neighborhood.

Cassie walked up confidently to the doors and knocked—three slow heavy thuds. From the other side, three slow knocks answered.

Cassie knocked again, this time a new rhythm—*rat-tatat-tat-tat*. Two sharp knocks answered and then—*click*. Cassie pulled the doors open and ushered Jessica through them before following her. The door slammed shut behind them, and the lock clicked back into place.

The Shifter Outreach Program

Dear Diary,

Hannah disappeared.

No one's talking about it. We aren't supposed to. We're just supposed to pretend that everything is normal. That there isn't suddenly a vacant seat in homeroom.

There are still whispers in the halls. Some are saying she ran away. Others say she's a Shifter and she was sent to the SRC. Both are high probabilities. A lot of my classmates are saying running is better than being sent There.

Jess got in huuuuge trouble at school today. Her class had career day, and Jess refused to do the worksheet. Apparently, she told the teacher to her face *that it's "stupid to get excited about a career that we might not even get to do." Mom and Dad are furious. They lectured* both *of us (Thanks, Jess!) about how "our family hasn't been tainted with a Shifter in over three generations" and "It's that kind of negative thinking that brings misfortune into our neighborhood."*

Jess had that obstinate look on her face, and I elbowed her in the side to shut her up. Our parents didn't notice, thank God. Jess is grounded for the whole weekend for talking back to her teacher.

I don't feel very good. I've been getting a lot of headaches lately. And my shoulders have been achy. Maybe I'm getting the flu.

Love Always,
Dani

Jessica shot up. Someone was yelling. She looked around, disoriented. A blonde woman across the room was screaming up at a lanky young man with curly dark hair. Her voice echoed off the cement walls, making it hard to understand what she was yelling about. Jessica heard the words "stupid" and "fuck" more than once.

Curiosity got the better of Jessica. She got up from her cot and approached cautiously. Their Shifter brands came into view as she got closer. The male Shifter towered over her, but still quailed at her fury.

"I'm sorry," Jessica heard him mumble before he turned and scurried away.

The Shifter woman turned and fixed her with icy-blue eyes. "You're the new girl."

Jessica shivered.

"Yeah, uh…" Jessica's words left her momentarily when a small fuzzy face peeked out from under the Shifter's hair.

"I'm Tia. This is Daya." Tia held out a hand to the fuzzy face and pulled her gently from her hair.

Jessica had never seen anything like it. It was long and lanky with a pointed face that ended in a delicate pink nose. Its legs were tiny compared to its body. Its fur ranged from white around its nose and ears to light brown across its back, all the way to dark-brown legs and a short tail.

"What is *that*?" Even as the words tumbled out of Jessica's mouth, she knew she fucked up.

Fury flashed across Tia's face.

"*She* is Daya, and *she* will be given respect." The "Or else" was unspoken, but definitely implied. Tia's eyes narrowed. Her muscles rippled under her shirt, like the fabric was barely containing it.

"I'm sorry, I just…I, uh, I've never…" Jessica babbled.

"Tia, you're not scaring away our newest recruit, are you?"

Jessica whirled around. Cassie strode toward them, followed by three others. All four of them bore Shifter brands. The other female stood taller than Tia and Cassie. She had a long face surrounded by messy dark-brown curls. The two male Shifters were easily over six feet tall. They both had black hair on the shorter side. One kept his bone straight and styled neatly, the other let his slightly longer hair fall in shaggy waves framing his face. They reminded Jessica of the Jung family that lived three doors down.

"Well, duh," Tia shot back emphatically. "If she can't handle being yelled at she doesn't belong here!"

A spark of spite-fueled anger shot through Jessica. The words tumbled out of her mouth before she could stop them.

"Hah! Like your little tantrum could scare me."

That was a mistake.

Tia's eyes blazed, and she thrust Daya at one of the male Shifters. One blink, and a pure white wolf was snarling in front of her. Its lips curled over long fangs, which glistened with saliva. Jessica stumbled back with a yelp, heart hammering.

"All right, enough!" Cassie stepped between Jessica and Tia. "Tia, if you can't play nice, then go find somewhere else to be."

Tia shifted back, and one of the male Shifters pulled his shirt off and gave it to her. Once she pulled it on, she shot Jessica a glare, took Daya back, and stalked off.

"Jesus girl, you had to pick a fight with *her*, didn't you?" the brown-haired Shifter said with a laugh. "I'm Heather by the way. He"—Heather pointed to the taller of the two following Tia out the door—"is Song, and he"—she pointed to the other—"is Chan-seong. Don't take Tia too personally. She's a good person, even if she does have a temper."

"That's an understatement if I ever heard one," Jessica muttered, still somewhat shaken.

Cassie and Heather laughed.

"C'mon, I'll show you around," Cassie chortled. "I doubt you remember much of what you saw last night."

That much was true. Upon entering, Cassie had introduced Jessica to the Shifter guarding the door. His name was already long gone. Cassie had then led Jessica up the stairs to the cot where she'd awoken. She fell asleep as soon as her head hit the pillow, despite the obvious stain on the cot. Cassie assured her that the cots and blankets and pillows were washed regularly because lice was often a problem in the colony.

"Can I ask what kind of animal is Daya?" Jessica asked timidly, not sure if these other women would have the same angry reaction at her not knowing.

"Of course, you can ask!" Cassie exclaimed. "Daya's animal form is a ferret. It's a type of weasel."

"Animal form? She's a—" Jessica didn't know how to end the sentence without offending them. She seemed to offend everyone these days.

"A Shifter?" Cassie finished for her with a smile. "Yeah, she is. Her and Tia, they're best friends. Tia's one of the only ones Daya trusts anymore."

"Why, what happened?" Jessica asked a little too eagerly.

"The SRC happened," Heather said darkly. "We were raided, and Daya was captured. When we finally managed to bust her out, she…" Heather took a deep breath.

"She wasn't the same," Cassie said quietly. "She'd scream in her sleep. Wouldn't talk to us. Wouldn't shift."

Heather nodded solemnly. "She stays in her ferret form most of the time now. If she doesn't come back soon—she might not be able to."

Jessica tried to swallow the lump that had formed in her throat. She didn't want to think of what could have happened to Daya to make her give up being human.

~*~

Cassie and Heather led Jessica through the warehouse. The air smelled like metal, old oil and—Jessica wrinkled her nose—*people*. Body odor, human waste, and ammonia hung heavy in the air. Shadows clung to the corners and high rafters. Lamps hung on the wall and flickered low in the dark. Most of the windows were sealed with plywood. The few that weren't had been slathered in black paint with thick, uneven strokes.

"We can't risk anyone seeing our lights," Cassie explained patiently when Jessica asked.

"We're already on the government's shit list," Heather said bitterly. "Just for demanding to be treated like humans."

Something flashed through her eyes that Jessica recognized too well. Layers of emotion—anger, fear, self-loathing, sadness at the situation they all found themselves in.

Jessica closed her eyes and wished in vain that she could go home. It wouldn't be the last time.

~*~

Jessica followed Cassie and Heather down the stairs to a huge common area. Once there, Heather excused herself, citing a need to pee.

Cassie led Jessica past clusters of Shifters—five or six in total. Jessica didn't bother to count. Quiet conversation mingled with laughter and the occasional animal sound: a bark, a hiss, shrill chirping. Jessica watched in awe as an older man, in his thirties if she had to guess, turned into a large crocodile. The low rumbling hiss that followed sent a shiver up her spine.

Jessica realized that Cassie was speaking and blushed. She hadn't been paying attention and missed the first part of the sentence.

"Learn to control your shift. Not just the process of shifting, but to control your animal once you've shifted. Your anima—"

"Wait, I thought you were supposed to be helping me get out of here? To Utopis," Jessica interrupted.

Cassie stopped and raised her eyes at Jessica.

"Of course, if that's what you want," Cassie said slowly. "But you have to understand that getting out of the country is not going to be an easy thing. There are several checkpoints between here and the border. It's going to take time to come up with a plan, get believable travel documents. Until we have everything you need, it's safest for you to stay here. And while you're here, you may as well learn how to control your animal."

Cassie brought Jessica to a group of Shifters. All three bore the telltale Shifter brand. The older girl looked vaguely familiar—Jessica couldn't quite place why. School maybe?

The boy was the one that Tia had yelled at not a half-hour earlier. He had a surly grimace and dark eyes that looked darker in the shade of his shaggy hair.

The younger girl had bouncing red curls and a wide freckly grin. Her mossy-green eyes sparkled in a way that irked Jessica for some reason.

"Jess, this is Sarah, Isaac, and Ashley. Sarah will be teaching you to shift."

Sarah smiled widely at Jessica, and Ashley gave her an enthusiastic grin. Isaac nodded curtly at her. He didn't smile. His tight expression mirrored the knot of anxiety in Jessica's stomach. A new feeling bubbled up under her anxiety. Friendship? Too soon. Comradery? Perhaps.

"Hi," Jessica managed to choke out. Why were her hands so clammy all of a sudden?

"I'll come back in a bit to see how you're getting on." Cassie grinned and gave a little wave as she walked away.

A beat of uncomfortable silence hung in the air around the group.

"Okay!" Sarah broke the silence. "So, Jessica, I assume you've never shifted before?"

Jessica shook her head. She could practically feel Isaac and Ashley staring at her. Her face flushed.

"That's completely fine. Some people take longer to find their animal than others," Sarah said gently.

"It took me like six months!" Ashley piped up.

Jessica fought to keep her face neutral. Even her voice was annoying.

"There's a few different ways of finding your animal," Sarah explained. "Sometimes they come to you in dreams. Sometimes walking out in the forest or on the beach brings them to the surface. Sometimes meditation works best. It's different for everyone, so don't get discouraged if you don't get it right on the first try."

"We were just about to go outside!"

Ashley's upbeat manner grated on Jessica's nerves. She scowled at Ashley when her back turned. *What if I don't want to find it?* Jessica didn't say it out loud. The thought echoed in her head. Somehow, she already knew—it wasn't an option.

The Doctor

Dear Diary,

Something's very wrong. I keep getting terrible cramps mostly in my hips and my shoulders. The other day I woke up and couldn't turn my head because the muscle in my neck seized up. The headaches are coming more often, and they take forever to go away. Five months till my birthday and the symptoms are getting worse. Harder to ignore.

Mom is suspicious. She keeps sneaking peeks at me when she thinks I'm not looking. I keep telling her I'm fine when she asks, but I don't think she believes me.

Jess barged into my room the other day and demanded to know what's wrong. I told her I had a headache and to beat it. She sat down on the bed and said she wasn't going anywhere until I told her what was actually wrong with me.

"There's nothing wrong with me except a nosy little sister," I snarked. The pain behind my eyes was just beginning to ebb away, and I wasn't in the mood to argue.

"Oh, come on," Jess snarked back. "You haven't been to the pool in three weeks."

How do I tell her?

"You've been crying in your sleep."

That was news to me. It would explain why I've been waking up with crusties around my eyes.

"I'm scared." Her voice was small.
I sat up and hugged her hard.
"Everything is okay, don't worry," I lied.
Yes, it's a lie. Everything's not okay. I'm scared too.
Please, God, let it be cancer.

Love Always,
Dani

~*~

Jessica sat with her back against a tree. Ashley sat across from her, babbling away about getting in touch with her "spirit animal," whatever that was. Jessica had stopped listening as soon as Sarah walked away to work with Isaac.

A month. That's how long Sarah had been bringing Jessica and Isaac outside to meditate. Yep, meditate. That's what Sarah wanted her and Isaac to do. Apparently, it would help them shift. That along with being outside in nature was supposed to help them connect with their inner animal.

"Just take a big breath in," Ashley took an exaggerated breath, looking expectantly at Jessica.

Jessica rolled her eyes and mimicked her, exaggerated and mocking. For some reason that Jessica couldn't explain, Ashley rubbed her the wrong way.

Ashley smiled, pretending not to notice Jessica's attitude.

"Then you exhale slowly and close your eyes."

Big exaggerated exhale.

Jessica let out her breath. This had to be the dumbest thing she'd ever done.

"Now keep your eyes closed and try to focus on your other senses. Think about what you can feel, what you can hear, what you can smell." Ashley took another deep breath.

Jessica grudgingly closed her eyes. If nothing else, she could pretend Ashley wasn't there. She took another deep breath through her nose.

A new sensation started to spread through her body. Each breath seemed to enhance her senses. The wind wasn't just rustling the branches.

She could hear each branch creak and clack together. The maple leaves made a different noise than the oak. Hardwood and softwood trees made different sounds as they swayed.

The smells hit her harder, though they took longer to register. First, she could just smell the damp earth in the forest. As she focused, she found she could identify the scents of each plant. A patch of wild mint captivated her momentarily. She could smell which trees were healthy and which trees were rotting on the inside. She could smell animal droppings nearby.

Jessica took another deep breath, eagerly this time. Another smell, unfamiliar but tantalizing, had captured her attention. It was wild and musky. Coppery and sharp. Something she needed. Her eyes popped open, and she stood, ready to find whatever it was that smelled so—

A shriek ripped out of her. Pain shot through her hands, up her fingers and into her fingernails, though she didn't know how her fingernails could hurt. She looked down at her hands in horror. Her fingers bent back and curled up under themselves. The cramp moved up through her wrist, forcing her hands to bend back. Her knees locked, and she fell forward with a cry.

"No, no, no. Oh please, God, no, no, no," Jessica whimpered. She was curled up on the forest floor. Her body was on fire. Her muscles rippled and stretched under her skin.

She was vaguely aware of Ashley yelling for Sarah. She could hear them talking around her, but she couldn't hear the individual words. Her heart pounded in her ears. She heard someone shouting her name. A guttural shriek ripped out of her throat.

Everything went dark.

~*~

Jessica was home sick from school, and her mother was fussing over her like she did whenever she or Dani got sick. She was cold and achy, like she had the flu. She was lying on the couch in her favorite jammies, snuggled under the big fuzzy blanket from her bed. Dani was sitting on the other end of the couch watching TV with her. She could hear the TV in the background. It sounded like the news, but the voices were distant, muffled.

Her mother set down a bowl of chicken noodle soup—the good box kind, not the slimy canned stuff that Dani liked. She sat down next to Jessica and stroked her hair the way she did when they were sick. She was humming, low and soft.

A wave of nausea swept over Jessica. She sat up and clutched her stomach.

"Mommy, I don't feel good," she whimpered pitifully. She looked over, but her mother wasn't there. She looked to the other side. No Dani. She was alone.

"Mommy? Dani?" Jessica called.

No answer.

The room darkened.

"Mommy?!"

Panic welled up as the room faded away.

"Dani!"

The walls faded away. Trees surrounded her. Her blanket dissolved and blew away in the breeze. The couch turned to stone and crumbled under her. The only things that remained were the muffled voices from the TV. The ground under her rumbled and shook. Jessica stumbled as fast as her aching legs would carry her. As she ran, the ground in front of her cracked open.

"Jess!"

Jessica's head snapped up.

Wyatt stood on the other side of the chasm waving her over.

"Wyatt!" she screamed, reaching for him.

The ground rumbled again and cracked open under her feet, and she fell, screaming, into the void.

~*~

Jessica's eyes popped open. She was lying on something hard. A car motor and the sound of gravel crunching under tires thrummed in her ears. She was in a car, that much was clear. In the trunk, if she had to guess. The last thing she remembered was pain. The blackout. Why was she here? Where were they taking her? Had the other Shifters sold her out? A bubble of panic welled in her chest as the worst-case scenarios played out in her mind.

Finally, after what felt like hours, the car slowed to a stop. Jessica felt them turn into what she assumed was a driveway. The motor cut out, and she braced herself. A few moments later the trunk popped open.

"You're awake!"

A wave of relief swept over her. Ben and Ellie smiled down at her. Ellie's baby bump had grown since she'd seen her last.

"What—?" Jessica started to ask as Ben helped her out of the trunk. They were standing in someone's garage. Tools were arranged neatly on a pegboard over a workbench. Two sawhorses held a half-finished rocking horse.

"You gave the ladies quite a scare, fainting like that," Ellie answered her unasked question. "They called us to get checked out."

"Checked out?" Jessica echoed, confused.

"Yep," Ben rumbled. "They said you got stuck mid-shift and fainted. Come on in, the doctor will be here soon."

Jessica followed Ben and Ellie into the house. The door from the garage led into the kitchen. A framed picture of Ben, Ellie, and the girls hung on the wall. They were at someone's wedding. The fridge was covered in drawings obviously done by the girls. Longing hit Jessica like a freight train. This was just what her family had been like when she was young. This is what she and Wyatt had dreamed of having.

"Come, sit," Ellie urged, steering Jessica to the couch.

Another family portrait hung above the fireplace. Pictures of the girls at various ages hung artfully around the room.

"You have a beautiful home," Jessica said as she sat down.

"Thank you," Ellie said graciously. "Let me get you something to eat. You must be starved."

Before Jessica could protest, Ellie waddled back into the kitchen.

"So," Ben said, sitting down across from Jessica, "you wanna talk about it?"

Jessica's face flushed crimson. "You didn't have to go to all this trouble. I'm fine, really."

"Really?" Ben stated skeptically. "'Cause people who are 'fine' don't get stuck mid-shift."

"I'm fine," she repeated stubbornly.

Ben raised an eyebrow. He didn't press her further, but she could see it in his eyes; he didn't buy it for a second.

~*~

Ellie came back into the living room twenty minutes later carrying a bowl of soup. Jessica's stomach and heart clenched at the same time. It was the good boxed kind.

"My youngest likes that kind," Ellie said as she set the bowl down. "I took a chance that you would be the same."

"Thank you," Jessica choked out. Tears pricked the corners of her eyes, and she blinked them back.

She ate slowly. Just as she was finishing up, the doorbell rang, and Jessica jumped out of her seat.

"That's just the doctor, relax," Ben said soothingly. He stood and strode to the door.

Jessica sat back down cautiously, but her muscles remained tense. Some instinct in her screamed at her to run, but she pushed it down. Ben had done nothing but help her time after time. She had no reason not to trust him.

The front door opened, and Jessica heard Ben greet someone loudly. A soft female voice floated into the living room.

Ben came back followed by a woman. Jessica couldn't have guessed her age if she tried. Her face was round and youthful, but there were tiny lines at the corners of her eyes and lips. Her wavy blond hair was just long enough to be held by a clip at the back of her head.

"This is her?"

The doctor had a thick accent that Jessica didn't recognize.

"Yeah," Ben said, smiling from behind the doctor. "Jess, this is Irina. She's a friend of mine. She's gonna check you out, okay?"

Jessica nodded slowly. Irina smiled gently down at her.

"Okay, Benjamin, you will give us privacy?" Irina asked pointedly.

Ben gave Jessica a reassuring smile. "We'll be in the kitchen if you need anything."

He and Ellie left, leaving Jessica alone with the doctor.

"So," Irina said, setting her purse down on the coffee table, "you gave everyone quite a scare, yes?" She pulled a stethoscope and a small first aid kit out of her purse.

"I guess," Jessica mumbled.

Irina began checking her vitals—heart rate, blood pressure with a portable blood pressure cuff, shining a small light in her eyes.

"Heart rate is elevated, but blood pressure is good," Irina stated almost to herself. "Pupils reactive. Thinner than I'd like, but that's to be expected. You are feeling pain? Nausea? Dizzy?"

"Uh, a little achy, I guess." Jessica scratched her arm absently. A couple of tiny half-healed cuts were just scabbing over and itchy as hell.

Irina nodded. "That is normal. Shifting is difficult, and getting stuck is more common than one would think."

"Why?"

Irina looked thoughtful as she put her things away. "The reason varies from person to person. Physical disabilities can hinder successful shifts. Malnutrition could also be a factor. A mental block is also possible. The SRC has found that sometimes genetic anomalies—"

"The SRC?" Jessica interrupted. Her eyes narrowed. "You—wait, do you work…there?"

"I do," Irina said plainly without missing a beat. "It is how I am able to help Shifters like you. Working there gives me access to research, equipment, medications—you need not worry."

"Does Ben—?"

"Benjamin is well aware." Irina packed her things back into her purse. She pulled a piece of paper from her purse. "You don't have any physical disabilities nor any injury from the failed shift. This"—Irina handed Jessica the paper—"is a list of breathing techniques. It will help with the anxiety."

Jessica took the paper warily. A thousand questions raced through her mind at once. *Do I trust this woman?*

Irina gave Jessica a gentle smile. "You are right to distrust. Enemies are everywhere. Even those who take care of us."

"I thought the SRC was the enemy," Jessica said slowly.

"An enemy, yes, but a useful one." Irina stood and looked down at Jessica. "You will never shift if you don't stop running from yourself. Take some time to rest and you will be fine."

"What if I don't want to shift?" blurted Jessica before she could stop herself.

Something flashed in Irina's eyes, something almost cold, calculating. It was gone before Jessica could name it. Irina's kind smile reappeared.

"That is a question only you can answer."

Irina stayed long enough to have a brief conversation with Ben and Ellie in the kitchen. Jessica heard them walk her to the door. As it opened, Irina warned Ellie loudly about the dangers of stress and too much exertion on the baby.

Jessica sat in the quiet living room, staring at the paper but not really seeing it. The paper felt heavy in her hands.

She drifted back to the night before Dani's test.

She had been fifteen, far too old to be running to her big sister in the middle of the night. But she did anyway. It was nearly midnight when Jessica crept to Dani's room. Flickers of light told her that her sister was still awake. Probably from nerves. She eased the door open and found Dani sitting in her bed, reading by flashlight.

"Hey, what are you still doing up?" Dani asked. She folded the corner of the page down to mark her place and closed the book.

Jessica climbed up on the bed with her.

"I'm scared," Jessica whispered. Tears pricked her eyes, and she blinked them away.

Dani pulled her into a tight hug. Jessica hugged her back, holding on to her for dear life. A little sob escaped before she could stop it.

"Shhh, it's okay," Dani comforted her.

"What happens if you test positive tomorrow? What are we gonna do?" Jessica whimpered.

"*We* aren't gonna do anything. *You* are gonna go back to school on Monday, and do your work, and get good grades, and marry Wyatt, and have a great life," Dani said firmly.

"But—"

"No buts. You are *not* going to ruin your life for me. I might not even test positive, so don't worry about it."

Jessica stayed in her sister's room that night. Dani had been gone when she woke up. A week later, her room was empty.

Ben returned a few minutes later carrying two mugs of hot chocolate. Jessica quickly wiped away a rogue tear.

"Don't tell Ellie," Ben said, winking at Jessica as he set the mugs down. "I'm not supposed to have sugar." He wrinkled his nose, and Jessica smiled, grateful for the return to normal, however brief.

"Where is Ellie?"

"Gone to pick up the girls," he said, sitting down in a worn armchair.

Jessica nodded. She let a beat of silence stretch between them.

"Did you know she works for the SRC?" Jessica asked. The question burst out of her.

Ben took a sip of his hot chocolate and set it down. "Yes, she does."

"Do you trust her?"

"I do…to a point."

"What does that mean?" Jessica asked impatiently. She hated when people gave vague answers or "beat around the bush," as her parents put it. "How do you know she isn't spying on you? Just waiting to turn you in for a big payout?"

"She very well could be," Ben said calmly. "Look, I get it, trusting people is scary. Irina has gotten us medicines that we couldn't get for ourselves. She's warned us about upcoming raids. She's never given me a reason not to trust her."

Jessica looked back down at the paper. She traced the edge with her thumb. Irina's voice still echoed in her head—calm, clinical. "She said I was running from myself."

"Are you?" Ben took another sip of his hot chocolate.

Jessica took a moment to take a huge gulp from her own cup, then sputtered as the hot liquid burned her tongue.

Ben chuckled, then looked thoughtfully at Jessica. "It's okay to be scared, you know. And it's okay to not want to shift."

"It doesn't feel okay," Jessica muttered, using her sleeve to dab at the chocolate droplets on her shirt.

"We live in a world where being yourself is dangerous. That's scary."

Jessica stared down at her hands clasped tightly in her lap. Finally, she looked up at Ben. "What do I do?"

Ben smiled. "I'll let you know when I figure it out."

Nomina Non Pereunt

Dear Diary,

Mom and Dad hosted a barbeque yesterday. Almost every family on the block was crammed into our backyard. The Jacobs and the Davises were the only ones missing. The Jacobs haven't come to community events since Sarah tested positive. The Davises have been shut up for two weeks now, since Hannah's disappearance.

Everyone has a different theory about what happened to her. Some say it was a kidnapping, or murder. I think she ran away before she had to be tested.

Would I have the strength to do that if it came down to it? I have no idea. I'd like to think so. But I still want to go to school. I can't do that without a clean Shifter test.

Wyatt came over this morning while Mom and Dad were out running errands. Jess wasn't home yet, so I sat with him while he waited. He's such a sweetheart. He talks constantly about how great my little sister is. He's absolutely convinced he's going to marry her someday.

At least, I know someone will be there to take care of her, if I can't.

Love Always,
Dani

~*~

Jessica's feet hit the floor of the tunnel with a soft *thud*. The scent of damp earth was a welcome contrast to the industrial smell of the city.

"You good down there?" Ben called after her.

"Yeah, I'm good."

"All right, I'm gonna head back now. Cassie'll be waiting at the end of the tunnel. You stay safe this time, you hear me?"

Jessica grinned and waved as Ben lowered the pulpit back over the mouth. Their journey had been almost uneventful—no patrols this time. The only bloodshed had been a scratch on her leg from a thornbush she hadn't seen in time.

Cassie met her at the mouth of the tunnel as promised. She looked Jessica up and down.

"You look like hell," she said gently, a quiet smile playing on her lips.

"Thanks, just what a girl wants to hear," Jessica shot back, smiling despite herself.

Cassie chuckled, and the two fell into step with each other.

"So how are you feeling?" Cassie asked as they tramped up the beach to the treeline.

"Better," Jessica answered simply. And it was true. Opening up to Ben had lifted a weight from her shoulders that she hadn't realized she'd been carrying.

"Good. You scared the crap out of us. The others will be happy to see you."

They lapsed into a comfortable silence. That's what Jessica loved most about Cassie: She didn't force conversation.

~*~

Jessica wasn't sure what she expected when they walked back into the hideout, but it definitely wasn't her being mobbed.

Heather met her first at the door with a loud, "You're back!" and a tight hug. Another Shifter—Nathan, she thought—clapped her on the back. Each time she was met with a hug or a handshake, a strange feeling fluttered in her stomach.

When Jessica finally managed to pull herself free from the others, she just had enough time to register a blurry figure flying at her before she was nearly knocked clean over. Ashley hugged her fiercely, sobbing into her shoulder.

"Oh, thank *God*, you're okay! You fainted, and then you wouldn't wake up, and I thought"—Ashley hiccupped and squeezed tighter—"I thought you were d-dead!"

Jessica stared at Cassie and Heather with wide eyes, both of whom were trying—and failing—to stifle their laughter. She patted Ashley awkwardly on the back. She felt a wave of guilt. Here Ashley was crying—*really* crying—and Jessica couldn't honestly say she'd do the same if the roles were reversed.

Maybe I was too harsh on her before.

"I'm okay now, no worries," she gasped as Ashley hugged her tighter. "But, Ash—?"

"Yeah?" Ashley sniffled.

"I can't breathe."

~*~

Jessica breathed a sigh of relief as she slipped through the door. She was flattered that everyone had been so worried, but she needed a few minutes of quiet. She'd managed to shake Ashley off, promising to hang out later.

A few steps in she realized that she was in a room she'd never seen before. It was tucked away off one of the common rooms, an inconspicuous door that she hadn't noticed. She took a few more steps, curiosity overriding her caution.

"You're back."

Jessica jumped out of her skin. Isaac was sitting with his back against the wall, half hidden in shadow.

"Yeah, uh—sorry," Jessica stammered. *Why was her mouth dry all of a sudden?* "Sorry, I won't bug you."

"You're not bugging me," Isaac grunted.

Jessica hesitated, then sat down, careful to keep a few feet between them. Somehow it felt almost like cheating, being this close to another boy.

"What was it like?" Isaac asked after a few moments of uncomfortable silence.

"I—what?" Jessica was flustered. She scolded herself internally, *Stop it. He's no different than anyone else. And you have Wyatt.*

"When you got stuck. Was—were you afraid?"

"Terrified," Jessica said. "I didn't know what was happening. It felt like something was trying to take over my body, and I couldn't stop it. It hurt."

Isaac didn't say anything at first, just nodded. Then he said, "Do you think it will hurt every time?"

"I don't know. I hope not."

Jessica took this time to look around the room. It looked like all the other common rooms, just smaller and emptier.

"What is this place?" she breathed.

Then she saw it.

Pictures. Hundreds of them. One of the walls was plastered with photographs. Each one held at least one Shifter. Most were smiling or laughing or making silly faces. All of them were young. Too young. Above the photographs the words *Nomina Non Pereunt*—Names Do Not Perish—were spray-painted. Scraps of paper, each bearing at least one name, hung beneath each photograph.

Jessica slowly rose, her legs suddenly unsteady. "What is this?" she whispered.

"Memorial wall," Isaac answered in a low voice.

Nausea overtook Jessica. There were easily thousands of pictures on the wall. One of the pictures closest to them held a boy that could have been Isaac's twin. The paper underneath read Jesse Hughes. His brother maybe?

A familiar name caught her eye: Hannah Davis. The Davis family lived in her neighborhood. Hannah's disappearance had caused a scandal that had lasted two whole months. Now here she was plastered on a memorial wall.

As she studied the pictures, she recognized more and more names. Greg, who was in her class, but was a year older than her. His parents locked themselves in their house for days after his test came back positive. Callum, who lived on the other side of Wyatt's house. He and Wyatt had been best friends. Suzanne from Dani's class. She'd disappeared much in the same way Hannah had, though her disappearance was overshadowed by Dani's positive test a week later.

Jessica's breath hitched.

Dani.

She touched the picture where her sister's face was frozen, mid-laugh. She sat between Sarah and another girl with frizzy black hair, all three making ridiculous faces at the camera.

Her eyes dropped to the paper underneath: It wasn't true. It *couldn't* be true.

Dani Hartford and Keisha Jenkins.

Jessica blinked, willed the letters on the paper to vanish, to rearrange into someone else's name. They didn't.

"Jess?" Isaac's voice was soft. Closer than she remembered. "Are you okay?

She turned slowly. Isaac was next to her, concern etched on his face.

"I...she...she was here," Jessica choked. "Dani. My...my...Dani."

The air felt thick. Her lungs wouldn't work right. Her vision blurred, and tears splashed unbidden down her cheeks. She didn't even push Isaac away when he wrapped his arms around her. She collapsed against him, sobbing into his chest. Hope she hadn't known she was holding on to crumbled into dust.

Her sister was gone.

~*~

Jessica stormed out of the memorial room. She had cried until she had nothing left. Isaac, to his credit, let her sob into his chest until she was done.

"I'll go get you some water," he offered, when her sobs had given way to hiccups. That was five minutes ago.

In that five minutes, Jessica's grief curdled into rage.

Her sister had been here. Her *sister* had been *here*—and no one had bothered to tell her.

She marched down the hall, each step fueling the fire in her chest. Nathan grinned and raised a hand in greeting—it died on his lips. His eyes widened at the unbridled fury in her eyes, and he scuttled away without a word.

Her sneakers slapped against the concrete floors. Her fists were clenched so tightly her nails bit into her palms.

How dare they.

How dare *they.*

As she rounded the corner, she bumped into Sarah.

Sarah, who had been in the photo with Dani.

Sarah, who Jessica now remembered from every one of Dani's swim meets. Her sister's best friend.

The memories clicked into place in an instant.

She had *known.*

"Jess, there you are," Sarah said, sounding relieved. "Isaac—"

Jessica's hand met Sarah's face with a sharp, echoing *crack!*

Sarah stumbled back with a gasp, her hand flying up to the reddening mark.

"*You!*" Jessica rasped, her voice shaking. "You knew, didn't you!"

"I…Jess, what—?"

"You *knew* Dani was here! You knew my sister was here, and you didn't *fucking* tell me!" She was shouting. She could feel people watching. A crowd formed around them. Good. Let them hear.

"Jess, I—"

"A month!" she screamed. "An entire month we've been together every *fucking* day! And you said *nothing!*" Jessica was breathing hard now. She wasn't normally one to swear, but damn did it feel good in the moment.

"What the hell is going on here?" Heather's voice cut through the commotion

Jessica whirled around. Cassie and Heather had pushed their way to the front of the crowd. Cassie's face darkened at the sight of the reddening welt on Sarah's cheek. Heather crossed her arms, jaw set.

"What happened to my sister?" Jessica demanded her voice low now, seething with rage. Her eyes were wild. "I want to know, and I want to know *now.*"

Files and Ferrets

Dear Diary,

Three more months until my test. I don't know how I'm going to make it. Mom is certain something is wrong now. Even Dad has noticed, I think. I've caught them talking about me when they think I'm not listening. They stop talking when I walk into the room. I can tell they're hoping the same thing: Please let us be wrong. Please let her be Normal.

They want it to be cancer too.

Jess and Wyatt are being sneaky again. I tried to ask Jess what's going on, but she won't tell me. She just keeps saying, "You'll see," and grinning at me. I'm so glad she has Wyatt. I don't know if I could live with having to leave if I was leaving her alone.

I've never been big on praying before, but I've caught myself doing it more and more.

Please, God, keep my sister safe when I'm gone.

Please, God, keep her from suffering this fate.

Love Always,
Dani

~*~

Jessica followed Cassie, Heather, and Sarah into a small room. A large map hung on a corkboard, color-coded pushpins stuck in at various points. Several roads were highlighted, and some were crossed out with big red *X*s. A file cabinet took up one corner of the room. Six chairs were strewn about the room haphazardly.

"Here, have a seat." Heather pushed one of the chairs toward Jessica.

Jessica didn't sit down. She was too angry to sit. She felt too much like a kid who had been sent to the principal's office. She paced restlessly, glaring daggers at the others.

There was a beat of uncomfortable silence. Cassie stared out the window. Sarah stared at the floor, wringing her hands. Heather was the only one who would meet Jessica's eyes. She leaned against the file cabinet, her arms crossed.

"Jess," Cassie said gently after a pregnant pause, "you have to understand, we never meant—"

"I don't care," Jessica growled, her fists clenched so hard her nails bit into her palms. "I don't want excuses. I want answers."

Heather straightened up, her jaw set. "Look, I get it, you're angry. But you will speak to us with respect."

"Really? Would that be the same respect you showed me when you lied to me for a whole month?" Jessica spat.

"Jess, we didn't lie to you," Sarah cut in. She reached for Jessica, who pulled back with a snarl.

"Jess, please," Cassie said calmly. "We had every intention of telling you about Dani. You were so exhausted when you got here. We just—we wanted to give you time to adjust before we dropped that on you."

Jessica crossed her arms, rage simmering just under her skin. "What. Happened."

"We went on a mission," Sarah said, her face contorting with guilt and agony. "Me and her and Keisha. Daya was captured. We went to get her back. We—" Her voice cracked, and she cleared it before continuing. "Keisha never made it. The guards—they shot her in the head. We made it to the yard. Dani—she was shot. In the leg. She gave me Daya and told me to go. I—" Sarah's voice broke, and tears silently streamed down her face.

Jessica stared, open-mouthed, at Sarah's tear-streaked face. Her heart pounded as she looked from Sarah to Cassie, then to Heather. Tears burned her eyes, and her chest tightened. Her knees threatened to buckle under her weight. She groped clumsily until she found a chair and sank into it.

"We went back to get her," Cassie said, her voice unusually thick. "But by the time we got there, she was gone."

"We got a hold of a bunch of their files," Heather said, pulling the file cabinet open. She pulled out a blue folder and held it out to Jessica.

Jessica took the folder with shaking hands. Her sister's name stared back at her in bold, block letters:

DANIELLE S. HARTFORD

She opened it.

Dani's picture was clipped to the front cover. Her face was gaunt, her cheeks hollow. One of her eyes was black and swollen nearly shut. She was sporting a bloody lip. Jessica skimmed the first page:

Shifter Rehabilitation Center
Shifter ID: 203-6405-HD86
CONFIDENTIAL

Subject	Hartford, Danielle Sophia
Genome	Shifter
Animal	Unknown
Father	Hartford, David Gerald
Paternal Genome	Normal
Mother	Sawyer, Pamela Muriel
Maternal Genome	Normal
Sibling(s)	Hartford, Jessica Marie
Sibling(s) Genome(s)	Unknown
Date of Birth	1999-01-16
Age	20 years
Height	5'7"
Weight	118 lbs
Status	DECEASED
Date of Death	2019-05-24

Cause of Death	[REDACTED]
Last Known Location	SRC Holding Facility C-13

Notes:
Subject was involved in incident C13-6412. Declared deceased after 30 minutes of submersion. Visual confirmation: Unavailable Body not recovered.

"But—this says they didn't find a body," Jessica said, her voice trembling. "Maybe—"

"I'm sorry, hon," Heather said softly. "It says she was submerged for 30 minutes. No one can hold their breath that long."

The room tilted.

The file slipped from her hands. Her hands were trembling, and her mouth went dry.

"It's not true," she whispered desperately. She looked up at Cassie, her eyes pleading.

Please, God, no. Not Dani.

"I'm so sorry, Jess. I—we did everything we could," Cassie said wistfully.

Jessica stood up unsteadily. The room was spinning. Her heart was hammering against her ribs. She couldn't seem to get enough air.

"I can't…I'm…I need to get out of here," Jessica blurted. Before the others could stop her, Jessica ran out of the room, down the hall, and out the door into the misty evening.

~*~

Leaves crunched loudly under Jessica's pounding feet. The cold night air swirled around her and burned her lungs. She ran deeper and deeper into the forest, away from the warehouse. Away from the ocean. Away from everyone. She didn't want their apologies… or their pity.

She couldn't face them. Couldn't face the truth.

Dani was gone.

She didn't stop until her legs threatened to give out. She sank against a tree, trembling and gasping for breath.

Dani.

Fresh sobs wracked her body. Jessica pulled her knees into her chest and cried into them. Unable to fuel her anger without a target to aim it at, it slowly ebbed away.

She wiped her face with the back of her sleeve. Leaning her head back against the tree, she could see a patch of stars through the canopy. She stared, seeing them and at the same time seeing nothing. Tears pricked her eyes as the memories she'd repressed for the last three years surfaced unbidden.

Dani in her swimsuit, holding her second-place trophy.

Dani scolding her and Wyatt for sneaking out.

Dani picking her up off the ground when she was learning to ride without training wheels.

Dani promising her that everything would be all right.

She let the memories come, one after another. A lump formed in her throat when she realized that she couldn't remember how Dani's voice sounded.

Jessica shivered. She regretted not grabbing her sweater. It was early December, and the night air was near freezing.

She supposed her old neighborhood was beginning to twinkle with Christmas lights. Mostly the boring white ones. Neighbourhood aesthetic and all that.

Jessica didn't know how long she sat there. It felt like hours. The cold seeped into her bones, and her butt went numb from sitting on the frozen ground. Just as she contemplated getting up and heading back, a rustling in the leaves caught her attention.

She staggered up, her frozen bones complaining all the way up. She groaned as blood rushed back to her butt, giving her pins and needles. She turned toward the sound, bracing herself.

A low, chittering noise drew her eyes down to the ground. Two beady eyes peered up at her. Jessica could just make out the outline of a long, furry creature standing at her feet.

"Daya?" Jessica breathed, squatting down.

Daya stood on her tiny back legs and chittered. Jessica slowly reached out her hand and picked her up gently. Her rough fur and warm little body warmed Jessica's hands slightly.

"What are you doing out here?" Jessica asked, cradling the ferret.

"We could ask you the same thing."

Jessica let out a shriek and nearly dropped Daya. Tia stepped from behind a tree, arms crossed, jaw tight. She wore a huge winter coat and was flanked by two massive black wolves.

"Jesus Christ, you scared me!" Jessica snapped, clutching Daya tight enough to make her yip. She loosened her grip and stroked the ferret's little head in apology. Daya dooked quietly.

"You're lucky that's all I did," Tia growled, stepping closer. "What the hell is wrong with you?"

Jessica blinked. "What—?"

"Do you think you're special?" Tia demanded. "'Cause you're fucking not!"

"Seriously, what—?"

"I'm talking about the huge fucking tantrum you threw before you ran out here in the middle of the goddamn night! Everyone is freaking out about you *again*!"

Jessica clenched her jaw. "You have no idea what you're talking about," she hissed, fighting to keep calm.

"I know that you're a spoiled fucking brat," Tia snapped. "And I know that you're a huge disappointment to everyone who knew your sister."

Jessica balked. "Don't you dare talk about—"

"Your sister actually fucking cared about the people around her," Tia growled. "All you can talk about is getting out of here. You don't care about us. You think you're the only one who's lost someone? Grow up."

"Look, I never want—"

"None of us wanted it. None of us." Tia's voice broke slightly, and for a moment, the fury in her eyes gave way to something different. Something raw...and painful.

A beat of tense silence passed between them. Jessica seethed, but beneath the heat, shame sat heavy in her gut. Tia was right. She *was* selfish. All she wanted was to get the hell out. And up until now she had been willing to use whoever was willing to help her.

"I'm sorry," Jessica said quietly. She swallowed hard to get the lump out of her throat. "I never…I didn't think—"

"That's your problem, isn't it?" Tia took another step forward. "You never think about anyone but yourself."

Jessica flinched, but didn't argue.

"You want to honor your sister? Keep her memory alive? Start giving a shit about the cause she gave her life for," Tia snapped.

Jessica nodded. She didn't trust her voice. Tears pricked in her eyes, but she blinked them back.

Tia wrinkled her nose at her, "Ugh, you're not gonna start crying again, are you? 'Cause I am *not* the right person for that crap. Cassie's the soft one. I'm just here to help you get your head out of your ass."

Jessica snorted out a laugh. "Does that…does that make you a proctologist?" Jessica sputtered between laughter.

Tia shot her a glare. "Let's go." She turned stiffly and strode off through the trees, the wolves melting into the shadows behind her.

Jessica followed, still snickering.

She couldn't be sure, but she thought she heard little chirps coming from her arms, almost like ferret laughter.

~*~

Jessica trudged after Tia through the gloom. The black wolves had vanished into the night as soon as the warehouse came into view.

"Oh, Jess, thank *God*!" Cassie met them at the edge of the trees. She threw her arms around her neck. Jess passed Daya to Tia, then hugged her back. She hadn't hugged someone—really hugged them—for so long. It felt good.

"Ugh, if you two are gonna get mushy about it, I'm outta here," Tia said, flipping her hair and turning on her heel.

"Hey, Tia?" Jessica called. "Thanks—for, y'know, pulling my head out of my ass."

"Yeah, well, don't make me do it again," Tia snapped.

A moment later, she disappeared into the trees.

"C'mon, let's get you inside, you're absolutely *freezing*," Cassie fussed over Jessica as they went inside.

Jessica reentered the warehouse, feeling something she hadn't felt in years.

It wasn't her old neighborhood. And it definitely wasn't Utopis.

But as the door clicked shut behind her, a thought flashed through her mind

It almost felt like home.

With Friends Like These

Dear Diary,

I can't take this anymore.

The headaches are relentless. It feels like little gnomes with pickaxes are tunneling through my skull. I'm surprised I haven't found any gray matter in my boogers when I blow my nose.

Worse than the headaches are the dreams. I keep dreaming that I'm in the middle of the pool, treading water. The waves get bigger and bigger and drag me under. No matter how hard I try I can't get back to the surface.

Then I see something—something huge. And fast. It swims at me, and I try to swim away, but I'm not fast enough. I always wake up right as it catches me. Every. Time.

I have started going back to the pool—mostly to keep Mom and Dad from worrying. I think I've managed to convince them that I just had a really bad case of the flu. Or maybe they just want everything back to normal.

Besides, being in the water makes the headaches go away.

I need to sleep, but I'm terrified. I know I'll see that thing again.

Love Always,
Dani

~*~

Jessica slept better that night than she had in over a month. Well, as good as one can sleep on a metal cot. She kept her eyes closed as she awoke, trying to hold on to her dream for as long as she could. The finer details were already slipping away.

It was a familiar dream—and yet, somehow, different this time. She remembered being in a forest. She was walking with…an animal? She couldn't remember exactly what it looked like. She remembered big, blotchy spots. And a long tail. And big amber eyes.

It took Jessica a moment to realize that, for the first time, she hadn't been running from the animal. She had strode alongside it as if it were an old friend.

She stretched leisurely and sat up, rubbing her eyes. Chinks of light filtered through the wood over the windows. Morning already. She got up slowly, stretching her taut muscles.

Pulling on a hoodie, she headed down to the main hall. It was mostly empty, just a few people scattered about.

"Jess!"

Jessica turned. Ashley was sitting at a table, waving her over enthusiastically.

Jessica almost made a face—old habits—but caught herself. Ashley could be annoying, but she hadn't done anything to deserve her spite. That lingering gut-feeling to mistrust her still bubbled under the surface. Jessica pushed it down.

She was tired of being alone.

Jessica crossed the room slowly, her arms folded against the morning chill.

"Hey," she said, sliding into a chair. "What d'you got there?"

Ashley fidgeted with the chipped mug of steaming liquid. "If I tell you, you have to promise not to say anything."

Jessica leaned forward, intrigued. She nodded.

"It's coffee."

The whispered words were barely audible, but Jessica perked right up. "You have coffee?" she squeaked. "How—?"

"Shhh!" Ashley hissed. "Do you want everyone finding out?"

Jessica clamped her mouth shut. Then, slowly, an impish grin spread across her face.

"I'll keep your secret," she said slyly. "For a price."

The color drained from Ashley's face. "What—?"

"I want a cup," Jessica said in a low voice. "I haven't had coffee in forever."

Ashley scowled, then pushed the mug across the table.

"You can have this one. I only took a sip," Ashley grumbled. "It's not even that good, just crappy instant."

Jessica cupped it, letting the warmth from the mug seep into her hands. It smelled like instant coffee, but in a place where coffee was scarce it was worth its weight in gold. She lifted the mug and took a drink, the hot liquid burning her tongue and throat on the way down. It was bitter and had a weird aftertaste. Warmth spread through her body, chasing the chill out of her bones. Jessica moaned in exaggerated ecstasy.

Ashley giggled. "You're so dramatic."

Jessica grinned back. "Where did you get this?" she asked, taking another gulp.

"Sorry, but if I told you, I'd have to kill you," Ashley said. Her expression was serious, but her eyes danced with mischief.

Jessica laughed. "Now who's dramatic?"

Both girls broke out in a fit of giggles. They lapsed into a comfortable silence. Jessica couldn't help remembering a time when it was her and Dani giggling together like that. She swallowed the lump that threatened to form in her throat.

"Isaac told me about your sister," Ashley said softly. "I'm really sorry."

"Thanks," Jessica grunted. She cleared her throat and pushed the half-empty cup away. "I'm gonna go…practice. Thanks for the coffee."

Before Ashley could protest, Jessica was up and heading to the door. She was willing to give Ashley a chance. But she wasn't ready to talk about Dani. Not with her. Not yet.

~*~

The days slowly melted into weeks. Jessica threw herself into helping keep the warehouse semi-livable. Like her, many of the new arrivals came from the factories in town. Some had been fired for being injured.

Some just left, unable to keep themselves alive on the meager payments offered by the factories.

Some came in with head lice. Anyone infested had their heads shaved, and the hair was burned in the fire barrel to kill the bugs. Jessica winced every time the shears were brought out. She swore, if anyone touched her hair, she'd kill them herself. She'd avoided the clippers so far—but not the smell of the thick chemical paste they used to kill the remaining eggs.

"You'll get used to the smell," Cassie said the first time Jessica gagged.

"You sure it didn't burn away your scent receptors?" Jessica asked, plugging her nose.

The bedbugs and fleas were worse. Everyone itched constantly. Jessica started helping Heather boil the blankets and pillows. She learned how to use a flashlight to find the bugs in the seams. The mattresses were treated with chemicals and thoroughly cleaned. They worked until their hands were pruny and raw.

"You sure you'd rather be in Utopis?" Heather teased one particularly rough day.

Jessica scowled at her. Her clothes were soaked. Dirty blanket water dripped from her bangs. "You did that on purpose."

Heather just laughed.

~*~

Jessica also threw herself into training. Cassie taught her basic hand-to-hand combat. She practiced with Ashley and Isaac almost daily.

Isaac had the advantage of height and reach. Something in the way he moved—measured, deliberate, powerful—made him a challenge. He could climb higher and faster than Jessica, and for the first time, she wasn't safe up in the branches. On the ground though, Jessica was quicker. She could outpace him, even with his long legs,

Ashley was another story altogether. She didn't look like a threat— that is, until Jessica let her get too close. The first time they fought, Ashley grappled Jessica and pulled her to the ground. She didn't let go until Jessica was gasping for air.

"Jesus, what *are* you?" Jessica gasped.

"My brother was on the wrestling team in high school," Ashley explained with a shrug. "I learned pretty quick how to defend myself. Not that it helped when my parents dropped me like trash."

Jessica blinked. The way Ashley said it like she was commenting on the weather, like it didn't hurt.

"Your parents…?" Jessica asked cautiously.

Ashley's smile didn't reach her eyes. "Normals. They let the SRC have me as soon as my test came back positive." She rolled her shoulder in a dismissive shrug. "Outreach broke me out a week later."

Jessica nodded knowingly. Her parents had done the same to Dani.

Along with combat training, Jessica pushed herself to shift. She meditated, walked through the woods. She did the breathing techniques Irina gave her. She chanted under her breath, her own personal mantra: "I *do* want to shift. I *do*."

But every time she got close, something inside her recoiled. The memory of the pain, the fear, the blackout pulled her back.

~*~

Every night, Jessica went back to the memorial wall.

At first, she only had eyes for Dani's picture. She stared at her sister's laughing face. Dani was her anchor, her link between her old life and her new.

"If you're out there, I promise—I *will* find you," Jessica whispered to her sister's picture.

As the days passed, Jessica found her gaze wandering.

She took in the other photos, memorizing the faces of those who'd fought a fight she wasn't sure she could fight. They were teenagers—boys and girls barely old enough to be called adults. Some made faces at the camera. Others grinned with arms flung around their friends, giving each other bunny ears. All of them were young. Too young.

They were just kids.

Jessica sat, staring at the wall of photographs, staring but not seeing. She was miles away, lost in her memories.

The first time she'd ever snuck out she was twelve. It was Dani who'd caught her sneaking back in.

"What the hell do you think you're doing?" Dani's whisper had been sharp and furious.

"None of your business!" Jessica hissed back.

"Of course, it's my business, you're my sister!"

"So?"

"You were out with that Armstrong girl, weren't you?" Dani accused.

Jessica clamped her mouth shut, grateful the dark hallway hid the flush rising in her cheeks.

"Ugh, Jess, do you have any idea how much trouble you'll be in when Mom and Dad find out?"

"They aren't going to find out," Jessica ground out. "Unless you're planning on snitching on me."

The memory blurred—the warmth of the hallway, Dani's crossed arms, the look of anger and disappointment in her face—and then faded.

"Jess?"

Jessica blinked. Isaac stood nearby, his eyes narrowed in concern.

"Oh, uh—sorry." Her voice cracked. She sniffled and quickly wiped her eyes. She hadn't even noticed she'd been crying.

Isaac didn't say anything, not right away. He sat down next to Jessica, stretching his long legs out with a quiet sigh.

They sat in silence for a few minutes. The only sound was the quiet hum of the generators and the murmur of conversation from the next room.

Jessica looked back up at Dani's picture and felt more tears roll down her cheeks. She let them. No sense wiping them away if she wasn't done.

"What was she like?" Isaac asked quietly.

Jessica took a shaky breath. "She was the best. She was kind and helpful—and a Goody-Two-shoes. Pain in the ass really."

Isaac chuckled. They lapsed back into silence. Jessica glanced over at Isaac. He was looking at the picture of the boy she assumed was his brother.

"What was he like?" She mirrored his question, nodding at the picture.

"I don't know," Isaac said with a sigh. "I don't remember him much. Our parents died when I was two, and we got put into separate foster homes."

"Oh, I'm sorry," Jessica replied, feeling suddenly awkward.

Isaac shrugged. "S'not your fault."

Jessica let her gaze wander back to Dani's picture. "I used to think if anyone was going to change the world, it would be Dani. She was the one who wanted to help people. I was just her trouble-making little sister with a bad temper."

"Bad temper? You? I don't believe it," Isaac teased gently.

Jessica pushed him away playfully.

It was nice, having someone to kid around with again.

"I think you could do it. You could change the world."

Jessica looked incredulously at Isaac. "Are you on drugs?"

"I'm not saying you have to be just like your sister," Isaac said, his face flushing pink, "You just—you're more valuable than you think."

Jessica's eyes widened as Isaac turned to face her. She became intensely aware of how close he was. She felt the heat of his leg against hers. His dark eyes glittered in the dim light of the lamp.

Her heart stopped when his lips met hers.

It wasn't like the crushing passionate kisses Jessica had seen time and time again in the movies. Isaac brushed her lips with his, hesitating long enough for her to pull away. Jessica was just as shocked as he was when she didn't. She melted into his lips, letting herself get caught up in the kiss.

Everything seemed to disappear. For that moment, nothing existed except her and Isaac. Her parents' rejection, Dani's disappearance, all of the misfortunes that led her here vanished in a puff of smoke. No one else existed—not Ashley, Cassie, Heather, Wyatt...

Wyatt.

The name hit her like a bucket of ice water. Jessica jerked back, her breath catching in her throat.

"I-I'm so sorry, I just...I have to go," Jessica stammered, already scrambling to her feet. She practically ran from the room, leaving Isaac frozen in place, wide-eyed and confused.

Oh, God, what did I just do?

Young, Wild, and Free

Dear Diary,

Something amazing had happened!

There's just over a month left before my birthday and the headaches, cramps—all of it—is gone! I haven't even had a nightmare the past two nights!

I did some research this morning, not wanting to get my hopes up. Apparently some Normals will develop hysterical symptoms, especially if a lot of people in their lives also start exhibiting symptoms. This isn't always the case, of course, but there's a good chance that's all my symptoms were.

I'm so excited! Now I can go to college like I planned!

Mom and Dad both seem happier since I've gotten better. Mom was even humming while she cleaned yesterday. She hasn't done that in months.

Jess got caught sneaking out to go see Wyatt last night. She tried sneaking out through the window, and it got stuck. When she forced it the rest of the way, it made a sound like a dying cat and woke up Mom! Boy, did she get in trouble. She's grounded for the next week, and Mom told her if she caught her sneaking out again she wouldn't be allowed to see Wyatt anymore.

Mom's calling me for dinner. She made my favorite to celebrate.

Love Always,
Dani

Jessica huffed impatiently.

She was sitting under a tree wrapped in a blanket. The early spring sun filtered through the bare branches, but it brought little warmth. The ground was cool and slightly damp beneath her. Buds were beginning to push their way out along the branches above her, and small birds twittered above her head—signs that the world was waking up after months of the gray stillness of winter.

Spring was always Dani's favorite season.

Jessica let her mind wander, giving up on meditation for the moment. Her thoughts buzzed like insects through her mind. She drifted back to a time when she sat under a similar tree with Dani. They giggled together and made flower crowns out of dandelions.

"I crown thee, Queen Danielle!" Jessica proclaimed, giggling and placing her lopsided crown on Dani's head.

Dani beamed. "And I crown thee, Queen Jessica!"

A nearly perfect flower crown adorned Jessica's head, and both girls broke out in a fit of giggles.

The memory faded, followed by another under that same tree years later. She sat with Wyatt. It was the day after Dani's eighteenth birthday, and she was crying uncontrollably. Wyatt held her, comforted her, promised her he'd always be there for her. It would all be okay. They promised each other on that day that they would run away together as soon as they were eighteen, Normal or not.

So why had she kissed Isaac?

Jessica dragged herself back to the present with a groan. She rubbed her face in her hands, then dragged them up through her hair—or what was left of it. Her lovely, long brown locks were gone, victim to a lice outbreak at Christmas. It was just long enough now that she could style it so she didn't look like an eight-year-old boy.

The question of Isaac settled heavy in her chest. It'd been two weeks since the kiss, but that didn't help lessen the guilt. Or the confusion. On one hand, she'd made promises to Wyatt. On the other hand, Isaac was there, and Wyatt wasn't. Could it be cheating if she hadn't seen him in over six months? Was he even looking for her? Or had he given up and she was holding on to a dream that would never come true?

Jessica sighed and leaned back against the tree, staring up between the branches. Obsessing over it was getting her nowhere—but she couldn't get it out of her head.

"Jess?"

A voice pulled her back to the present.

A twinge of unease curled in her belly as Ashley approached. Jessica pushed it down. Though she'd made the conscious decision to befriend her, her instincts still nudged at her to be careful.

"I thought I'd find you out here," Ashley said, plopping down next to her and offering a small package wrapped in a paper napkin. "Heather made muffins again." Ashley wrinkled her nose as Jessica took the muffin. "It's not bad if you rip off the burnt part."

Jessica snorted and turned the muffin over. She slowly picked away at the burnt base.

They sat for a few minutes, eating in companionable silence. Ashley picked at a loose thread on the sleeve of her hoodie.

"So...I hear you and Isaac are a thing now," Ashley said casually, watching Jessica's face closely.

Jessica choked on a bite of muffin. She coughed violently. "What?! No!"

"Are you sure? It's just"—Ashley leaned in conspiratorially—"Isaac told me you guys kissed."

Jessica felt the blood drain from her face. "What?" she asked, her voice suddenly hoarse.

"He...he told me you guys kissed," Ashley repeated hesitantly, squirming uncomfortably.

Jessica's fists clenched, crushing the half-eaten muffin. Her shock slowly gave way to anger, and she felt her face beginning to flush.

"He told you that?" Her voice was low, dangerous.

"Y-yeah, but—"

"How *dare* he!" Jessica shot to her feet, momentarily at a loss for words. "How *dare* he!"

"Jess, look—don't be mad at him. I forced it out of him," Ashley pleaded.

Jessica wasn't listening anymore. A white-hot wave of betrayal roared through her. He hadn't promised her silence, but the fact that he went behind her back...

Her pulse pounded in her ears. Her clenched fists shook, her nails biting into her palms. It was too much. It was just too...

She gasped.

Her muscles pulled and twisted under her skin. Her fingers curled back, and her knees buckled under her. A billion tiny pinpricks washed over her in waves, and she watched in fascinated horror as black and gold fur sprouted over her arms and hands. Her fingernails grew and curved into inch-long claws.

It was over almost as quickly as it began. Jessica stood up on her huge paws. Her senses were instantly overwhelmed. She could smell *everything*. The moss, the trees, the earth, animal droppings, animals. Her ears twitched and swiveled at every sound. She could actually *feel* things moving through the earth. A herd of nearby deer trampled the ground, making little tremors that Jessica felt through her feet.

"Holy shit," Ashley breathed, taking a step back.

Jessica turned her head toward her. She was a big cat, though which one she had no idea. Identifying animals wasn't exactly something they taught in schools, beyond Shifter identification. Big splotchy spots covered her body, deep golden fur with broken black outlines. Inside the bigger splotches, small black spots were scattered like splattered ink. She would later find out that it was called a jaguar.

Jessica took a hesitant step. Then another. A jolt of sensation up her spine startled her and made her whip around. Nothing. Another jolt a second later made her growl and jump. The more agitated she got, the more jolts shot up her spine. It took her longer than she would admit later to realize it was her tail.

Her anger drained away quickly after the shock of her first shift. A new sensation washed over her. Strength. Power. Control. The irresistible urge to run—not away from anything, just to *run*—overpowered her. She turned on her heel and took off, leaving Ashley to shout at her to come back. She ignored her.

She was young, wild, and free—and for the first time in a long time, she was *alive*.

~*~

Jessica didn't know how long she prowled. Time meant nothing to her big cat self. She wasn't just Jessica anymore. She was a power. Muscle. Movement. A shadow stalking through the forest.

And stalk she did. She crept up on the herd of deer, months of malnutrition driving her jaguar to fill her belly. The only thing that kept her from succeeding was the wind. It shifted at the last second, coming in from behind her and wafting her scent right to the herd. They scattered, leaving her scrambling. She let out a frustrated huff. She had to settle for splashing into a nearby creek, catching fish and devouring them until she was satisfied.

When the gnawing hunger dissipated, she flopped down on a flat, sun-warmed rock. She licked the water from her coat, paying close attention to her paws. Only once she was satisfied with the cleanliness of her coat did she stop to take stock of her surroundings.

She was at the edge of the creek, sunbathing in the one spot where the sun could penetrate the canopy. Her tail flicked lazily, her breathing syncing with the sounds of the forest. A frog croaked. Birds chirped all around her. A faint breeze rustled through the trees. The forest stretched before her, promising freedom—freedom from responsibility, from pain, from death—if only she would give in. If only she would abandon her human side and let the jaguar rule.

Don't let it get the best of you, Jess.

The sentence caught her off guard. Her tail flicked nervously, and she peered through the trees. Nothing seemed out of place, no humans or animals near enough to cause her anxiety.

You are Jessica. You are in control.

Jessica stood up. She breathed deep, searching for an out-of-place smell. Her ears swiveled back and forth, straining to hear where the voice was coming from.

Take control, Jess. The others need you.

Jessica blinked. Slowly, their faces swam into view. Song. Chanseong. A boy named Curtis she'd met at Christmas.

The jaguar in her growled.

Sarah. Nathan. Tia. Daya.

Jessica took a deliberate step, turning to face where she'd come from.
Isaac. Ashley. Cassie. Heather.

The jaguar growled again, and she halted.

Dani. Wyatt.

The jaguar stilled.

Jessica dashed through the woods, back toward the warehouse.

~*~

Jessica padded into the clearing behind the warehouse, paws heavy
with exhaustion. The jaguar still tugged at her—pulling, urging,
whispering of trees and freedom. She pushed back, clinging to the
human names that had brought her here.

Dani. Wyatt. Isaac. Cassie.

She circled to the back entrance—then stopped.

How was she supposed to knock? She stared at the door, then let
out a low, frustrated whine.

To her surprise, it creaked open.

Cassie stepped out cautiously, a blanket folded in her arms. She
scanned the trees, keeping her movements slow and calm. The door
clicked closed behind her.

"Jess?" she asked softly. "Jess, is that you?"

Jessica huffed and tried to growl out a yes—but all that emerged were
guttural, garbled roars. She stomped a paw, then flopped dramatically
to the ground with another grunt.

Cassie flinched, just slightly, then caught herself and let out a shaky
laugh.

"Okay, okay," she said gently. "I need you to focus. Picture yourself—
your human self. Will it back."

Jessica closed her eyes. She tried to picture her face.

Nothing.

A low, mournful whine escaped her throat.

"It's okay," Cassie said. Her voice was steady now. "I know it's hard.
Just breathe. In…and out. That's it."

Jessica obeyed. She drew in a deep breath through her wide,
twitching nose, then let it out slowly.

A flicker of memory surfaced.

Sitting beneath a tree. Ashley telling her to breathe, of all things. Jessica rolling her eyes, muttering—

This is stupid.

Her body jerked.

A strangled sound tore from her throat as her limbs twisted. Claws shrank. Her fur melted away. Her tail withered and curled into nothing. Her teeth retracted, her bones cracking as they rearranged.

And then—

She was human.

She stood up, naked, shaking and gasping.

Cassie was already there, wrapping the blanket around her shoulders. Her smile was wide and proud.

"Welcome back."

Cassie led Jessica to the cafeteria and sat her down at one of the tables. She shivered under her blanket while Cassie went to the kitchen to make her something hot to drink. Her joints felt weird, like they needed to be cracked. Her whole body tingled and itched—remnants of the shift. Would every shift be like this? Jessica shuddered at the thought.

Cassie came back a few minutes later and set a steaming mug down in front of her. The liquid inside was…brown?

"Uh, thanks?" Jessica said, raising an eyebrow at the brown liquid.

Cassie laughed. "It's beef broth. We managed to score a case on our last raid. It'll help, I promise."

Jessica picked up the mug skeptically. She used the blanket to hold it without burning her hands. She sighed and just sat for a moment, soaking in the heat. She took a shaky sip and sighed.

"Jess!"

Jessica turned to see Ashley barreling toward her. Unease coiled in her belly. She took another sip, letting the salty broth steady her stomach.

"I'll give you guys some privacy," Cassie said with a knowing smirk. "I'll come check on you later. Make sure you drink *all* that broth."

Ashley skidded to a stop as Cassie walked away and plopped down across from Jessica. Her eyes were wide and she was practically trembling with excitement.

"That. Was. So. *Cool*," she gushed, grinning so wide Jessica was sure her face would split open. "You *shifted*. Like full-on *shifted*. Into a *jaguar*!"

"Huh. So that's what it's called," Jessica mused.

"You were *awesome*—all sleek and fierce, Miss Don't-Mess-With-Me-I-Have-Claws. Total predator queen."

Jessica snorted. Her broth sloshed dangerously in the mug. "Predator queen?"

Ashley leaned in, lowering her voice. "I was thinking, we need to celebrate this."

Jessica raised an eyebrow. "Celebrate? You mean like a party? You do know we live in a bug-infested warehouse, right?"

"No, not like a party," Ashley's grin widened, if that was possible. "Like a *run*. You, me, maybe Curtis, Nathan, Isaac—" Ashley broke off at the sour look that crossed Jessica's face. "Or maybe not Isaac. Just us and the forest. No trainers breathing down our necks. What do you say?"

Jessica hesitated. Her body ached in places she didn't even know she had muscles. But the jaguar in her—it wanted to *run*.

"Are you sure it's safe going out in a group like that? Should we tell someone where we're going?" Jessica asked slowly.

Ashley waved a hand dismissively. "We'll be careful, don't worry. We're just a small group. No trails, no roads, just running. What do you say?"

Jessica gulped back her broth, burning her tongue in the process. "Let's do it."

~*~

It was past midnight when Jessica pulled on her baggiest hoodie. She was nearly to the top of the stairs when a low voice startled her.

"Where are you going?"

Jessica whipped around. Isaac stood in the door, his eyes glittering in her flashlight. Her face hardened

"None of your business," she snapped.

Isaac blinked in confusion. Before he could say anything, Jessica turned her back on him and rushed down the stairs.

She wouldn't have that fight tonight. Tonight was going to be a good night.

At the bottom of the stairs, she met Curtis. They were joined by Nathan a moment later. The three snuck down toward the exit and peered down the hall. Tia sat at the guard post, reading a beat-up book.

"How do we get past her?" Curtis breathed, making as little noise as possible.

"This way."

Ashley, appearing out of seemingly nowhere, beckoned for them to follow her. She led them down to the laundry. A row of ancient washing machines lined one wall. A sheet of plywood hung behind each machine.

"There's a crawlspace behind one of these machines," Ashley whispered. "I heard Cassie and Heather talking about it once. It's an escape route—in case we ever get raided."

Nathan groaned. "A crawlspace? Really?"

Ashley crossed her arms. "Unless you'd like to sneak past Tia."

Jessica and the boys glanced at each other. As unappealing as a crawlspace may be, getting caught by Tia was worse.

Ashley wriggled in behind the machines and tested the wood behind each one. Behind the fourth machine, the wood came off with a soft *click*.

"C'mon," she whispered.

Jessica, Curtis, and Nathan followed her into the cramped space. It was less a crawlspace and more a tunnel, obviously meant for the smallest people to escape through. Jessica was soon covered in dirt from head to toe.

A few moments later, they emerged in the shadow of a massive pine tree. Its lower limbs brushed the ground, hiding the tunnel mouth from anyone who may be looking for it. Jessica brushed the dirt off her face and grinned at Ashley.

"Shall we?"

They separated before their shifts, the boys going around one side of the tree and the girls staying on the other. Jessica stripped down, shivering in the cool night air. She folded her clothes and pushed them back under the tree. When she shifted back, she'd have something to wear.

She closed her eyes and focused on the jaguar—the feel of its muscles rippling under her skin. The shift came faster this time, easier. A few seconds later, she was stretching her feline muscles.

She looked around for the others. An animal like a small wolf trotted around the tree and yipped at her. A large lizard rode on his back. A rustle under her feet drew her eyes down. A six-foot-long snake wound its way through the underbrush. It disappeared under the tree.

Jessica felt a thrill rush through her, bringing emotions that she hadn't felt in months.

They were *young*.

They were *wild*.

They were *free*.

Jessica and Curtis romped through the forest, paws leaping deftly through the moss and leaf litter. Nathan followed close behind, his muscular lizard body weaving expertly through the roots and branches with surprising agility.

Jessica pounced on Curtis, sending him rolling across the forest floor with a yelp. Nathan scurried onto a rock, tilting his head to watch the two playfully snap at each other.

Ashley slithered alongside now and then, a green blur in the undergrowth, barely visible at times. She couldn't keep pace with them for long, but she made up for it with stealth, often appearing ahead of them when they least expected it.

Jessica's jaguar was practically purring. She reveled in the freedom of the night. She bound away from her friends, inviting them on a chase through the moonlight.

Then the wind changed.

A new scent, foreign to the forest but familiar—oh so familiar—to Jessica. She leapt away, racing toward it. She heard Curtis yip at her in confusion. She could hear him following, but he couldn't keep up with her pace.

Her pulse pounded in her ears. It couldn't be. There was no way. She burst through the trees—

And stopped in her tracks.

Staggering through the underbrush, ragged and exhausted, was Wyatt.

Wyatt.

Jessica stared at him, not daring to believe her eyes. She heard Curtis clamber up beside her, then Nathan.

Jessica surged forward, forgetting for the moment that she was a very large, predatory cat. Wyatt cried out when he saw her and stumbled back, tripping on the roots of a large tree.

She stopped, hurt for a moment at the fear in his eyes. Then a flick of her tail reminded her what she looked like. She took a deep breath, focusing on holding him in her arms—her human arms. A moment later, she stood up.

"Jess?" Wyatt's voice was hoarse. He scrambled up, his face changing swiftly from disbelief to relief, then to utter joy. He took a step toward her.

A spotlight flicked on.

Then another.

Then another.

"*There!*" a shout rang out nearby. Soldiers swarmed through the trees like hornets, weapons trained on Jessica.

Then all hell broke loose.

Difficult Decisions

Dear Diary,

Two weeks, two weeks, two weeks*!*

It's been two weeks since my last headache. It's just over two weeks till my test. I'm so excited. I spent so long thinking I wasn't going to get to go to college. I can't believe it! I keep waiting for the headaches and the nightmares to come back, but they haven't. Not even a twinge!

Mom says I'm "right back to my old self again." She even gave me and Jess and Wyatt money to go to the movies. We went, and then spent the rest of the afternoon goofing off at the mall.

I'm so close now. I know it's silly, but it feels like a sign. I'm meant to do something great with my life. College will be the first step, and then who knows? Maybe I'll make a big discovery and make a difference.

Jess is back to her old self too. I don't know who's happier, me or her. She's been watching the mail like a hawk for some reason. She won't tell me what she's waiting for though. She says I'll "see after I've passed my test." What a goober.

To paraphrase Browning, "The symptoms have passed, all is right in the world."

Love Always,
Dani

~*~

It was absolute chaos.

The floodlights swept through the trees, looming shadows and blinding light flashing in Jessica's eyes. Soldiers shouted over one another, their voices echoing through the woods until it was just a wall of noise.

Nathan vanished into the undergrowth with surprising speed. Curtis yipped and bound after him—but not fast enough. A volley of tranquilizer darts flew through the air. One struck home. A sharp yelp reached Jessica's ear, and she turned just in time to see Curtis stagger a few unsteady steps, then collapse.

The soldiers surged forward, surrounding Wyatt. He threw his hands up, eyes wide with fear.

Jessica snarled and shifted, the jaguar rising to the surface like a tidal wave. In seconds she was on four paws again, muscled and menacing. She leapt in front of Wyatt, her roar ripping through the noise and stopping the soldiers cold.

"Fire!" a panicked shout rang through the air.

They cocked their guns —

A scream rang out as a soldier went down, tackled by a second large, spotted cat. Jessica barely registered that it wasn't a jaguar like her—the build was different, leaner. It was a leopard—Isaac, she'd later realize.

The clearing erupted.

Two black wolves charged in, followed by a blur of white—Tia, Song, and Chan-seong. They moved as a unit, black and white fur weaving together in a deadly rhythm. Song and Chan-seong flanked the soldiers, snapping at their heels, driving them inward. Tia struck like lightning, bursting from the shadows to tear into exposed throats.

Jessica followed suit, leaping at the soldier nearest her. He went down under her weight, his gun pinned beneath her paws. She grabbed his neck in her jaws and bit down, the bones shattering with a satisfying *crunch!*

But the numbers kept growing. More soldiers poured through the trees. Tranquilizer darts hissed past her head. The tide was turning.

A sharp howl pierced the air—Tia's signal.

Retreat. Or be taken.

Jessica turned, reluctantly bounding into the shadows. Darts thudded into trees around her. She turned back and saw Wyatt run a short way, then stumble and fall. Two soldiers rushed him. They hoisted him to his feet, and one jabbed a needle into his neck. They carried him off into the night.

She hesitated, her instincts screaming to run back and save him. Another dart whizzed past her ear. Isaac appeared beside her, a loud warning growl urging her to run.

So she ran, weaving expertly through the trees. The image of Wyatt, limp in the soldiers' arms, burned behind her eyes.

~*~

Jessica stumbled through the door, held open for her by Heather, still disoriented from rapid shifting. She collapsed a few steps in, landing near Ashley, who was white and shaking. Nathan sat next to her, his eyes haunted.

Isaac, Tia, Song, and Chan-seong piled in moments later. They were breathing hard and sporting minor wounds of their own. Isaac and Chan-seong were supporting Song, whose leg was bent at an awkward angle. Isaac's dark eyes were bruised and nearly swollen shut. Chan-seong was bleeding from a deep gash on his shoulder.

Last through the door was Cassie in owl form. She swooped in and landed next to Tia as Heather slammed the door shut. Seconds later, she was human again.

"Set him down here," Cassie ordered quietly.

Isaac and Chan-seong laid Song down, and Heather rushed forward with a first aid kit.

"Jess, Ashley, go find something we can use as a splint."

Jessica forced herself up and pulled Ashley along with her.

They stumbled into a nearby office. Jessica dove to the desk, searching frantically for something, anything that could be used as a makeshift splint. Ashley sank down into a chair near the door.

"They shot at us," Ashley said in a shaky voice. "They—they tried to kill us."

Jessica stopped and stared at Ashley, whose wide, unseeing eyes were fixed on the wall.

"They were tranquilizer darts, Ash."

Ashley didn't make any sign that she heard Jessica.

"They got Curtis," she whimpered. "They shot him."

"With a *tranquilizer* dart. He's not dead."

"This is all my fault," Ashley moaned, burying her face in her hands.

"Fine," Jessica snapped impatiently. "Fine, you're right. It's all your fault."

Ashley's head snapped up, her mouth open in shock. Pain and fear flickered through her eyes.

"I don't have time to babysit your feelings," Jessica said bluntly. "You wanna sit there and throw a pity party? Have at 'er. Curtis is in danger. *Wyatt* is in danger." She grabbed an overturned office chair and yanked off one of the legs.

"I just wanted to have one fun night," Ashley whispered.

Jessica clenched her teeth. With a strength she didn't know she had, she pulled another leg free. She stormed out without another word.

~*~

Jessica rushed back into the hall, her anger fizzling quickly at the sight of her injured friends. She handed the chair legs to Heather, who was crouched beside Song, wrapping his twisted leg. Cassie was cleaning Chan-seong's shoulder, her hands slick with blood. Isaac was sitting near them, his swollen eyes closed and his head resting on the wall.

Jessica stepped toward him—

Wham!

Something slammed into her shoulder, hard. The world tilted. The next second she was pinned to the wall.

"*Traitor!*" Tia shrieked.

Her face was wild, eyes blazing, lip split and bleeding again. Her forearm crushed Jessica's throat against the wall.

Jessica clawed at Tia's arm, lungs burning. Black dots danced at the edge of her vision.

"Tia! Tia get off her!" Heather shouted.

Cassie and Heather were on her in seconds, dragging Tia back. Jessica collapsed, coughing, knees hitting the concrete floor *hard*.

"*This is your fault!*" Tia screamed, her voice ragged as she gestured around her. "*You led them into a trap!*"

"I-I didn't…" Jessica wheezed, still trying to pull air into her lungs. Her throat burned where Tia's arm had crushed it. Isaac, who had scrambled back up when Tia started yelling, stepped between her and Jessica.

"*Look at them!*" Tia shouted around him, her voice cracking. "*Look at what you did!*"

"I didn't know it was a trap!" Jessica tried to shout back. It came out as a croak. She pulled herself to her feet.

Tia ground her teeth. "Then you're just stupid."

"Okay, that's enough. Tia if you can't be helpful, then go somewhere else and calm down," Cassie said firmly.

Tia was shaking with fury. She opened her mouth to argue.

"It wasn't her idea. It was mine."

Ashley's voice stopped them all in their tracks. Everyone turned. She stood a few feet away, arms wrapped around herself.

"It's not Jess's fault. It's mine," Ashley mumbled, head hanging with shame.

Tia stepped toward her, fists clenched. Heather stepped deftly between them.

"There's no point in playing the blame game," Heather said matter-of-factly. "It's done now. All we can do is regroup and come up with a plan."

"Okay, I'm in. When do we leave?" Jessica asked.

"What makes you think you're coming?" Tia snapped.

Jessica set her jaw, determination etched on her face.

"I haven't waited this long to see Wyatt again just to lose him now."

"We understand that. But, Jess, we can't just rush in half-cocked and expect to get him *or* Curtis back," Cassie explained gently.

"So what? We just wait around for them to be killed?" Jessica demanded.

"Look, it's been a long night. Go to bed, try to get some sleep. We'll let you know as soon as we know anything," Heather said, going back to tend to Song.

Jessica didn't move.

"Go," Cassie said quietly, giving her a gentle nudge.

Jessica turned reluctantly and headed slowly up to bed. Tears pricked her eyes, and a lump formed in her still sore throat.

"Hey."

Jess stopped, halfway up the stairs. She closed her eyes and took a breath.

"What do you want, Isaac?" she said, her voice breaking.

"Just—don't do anything stupid, okay?"

Jessica turned to look at him. He was peering up the stairs through swollen eyes.

Guilt collected and swirled in her gut. Even now, he was still looking out for her.

And all she could think about was Wyatt.

~*~

Jessica didn't sleep.

She lay in the dark, eyes open, blinking back tears. Her thoughts looped incessantly, replaying the events of the night.

The lights.

The soldiers.

Curtis going down.

Wyatt with his hands in the air.

The fury in Tia's eyes as she screamed.

By morning, the air in the warehouse was thick with tension. Even those who hadn't heard the commotion the night before seemed to sense it. Chatter seemed to die off whenever Jessica entered a room. Sideways looks followed her everywhere.

Jessica cornered a weary Cassie shortly after lunch.

"No, Jess, we don't have any information yet. I'm sorry," Cassie said, her voice tired.

An hour later, she tried Heather. Same answer.

By dinner, Jessica's skin itched with frustration.

"How can you *still* not know anything?" she snapped.

"We're working on it," Heather said firmly. Her voice had an edge to it, one that warned Jessica that she was pushing it.

Jessica bit her tongue to keep from screaming.

She spent the evening prowling restlessly around the warehouse, snapping at anyone who crossed her path. A couple of newbies scurried out of her way, wide eyed and whispering something that sounded like, *"That's the one."*

She didn't care. Let them talk.

Sleep came in fits. Twisted nightmares of Wyatt being dragged away, beaten screaming her name jolted her awake again and again. Finally, around 3:00a.m., she kicked off her blanket.

She had waited long enough.

She crept down the stairs to the office where Cassie, Heather, and Tia planned their raids. Jessica searched through the papers scattered on the desk. Nothing. Filing cabinet? Locked.

Jessica swore under her breath.

She looked around the room, dejected. She was close to giving up when her eyes fell on the map.

A spark of hope flared in her chest. All she needed was an inkling, a clue, of where they were holding Wyatt. If only she knew what the pins meant—

A blue pin caught her eye. *Curtis* was penciled in next to it. Next to that a highlighted road that led to a red pin marked with a series of numbers. Then it clicked. The red pins scattered across the map—they were the SRC facilities.

Jessica leaned forward, studying the map intently, memorizing the route. If she could get back to the capture sight and turn right she could—

A noise at the door made her jump. Isaac stood at the door, eyebrows raised. The swelling around his eyes was nearly gone, but angry purple bruises were still visible.

"I thought you were supposed to wait," he murmured.

"I can't," Jessica whispered desperately, "I just—I *can't*. They have Wyatt. They could *kill* him."

Isaac ran his hand through his hair and sighed. He chewed on his lip when he was thinking, Jessica noticed. It looked like he was having some big debate with himself—

"Well, we better leave soon if we don't want to get caught."

Jessica blinked. "We?"

"You didn't think I was gonna let you do something this stupid on your own, did you?" he said. He took a step toward her...then another.

Jessica swallowed hard. She was suddenly very aware of just how tall he was. Her thoughts scattered as he stopped right next to her. They were almost close enough to touch. All she would have to do is reach out—

"It looks like this is the most likely place."

She snatched her hand back and shook her head to clear it. He was pointing to the red pin closest to Curtis's blue pin.

"Right," she said, stepping around him. Now wasn't the time to get distracted.

Wyatt.

She was going to save Wyatt.

~*~

Mist clung to the forest floor, a thick blanket wrapped around the trunks of the trees. Thick gray clouds hung low and threatening in the sky. Jessica and Isaac could both smell it. Rain was coming.

They had been searching for a couple hours already, completely relying on their sense of smell. Damp earth and animal droppings overwhelmed their noses. Every so often they caught a whiff of their friends, of themselves. They followed the scents as best they could, but they were already melting away with the mist.

They pushed on, two big cats wending their way through the woods. A low rumble in the distance urged Jessica to go faster. If it rained before they got there, any scent left behind would be washed away.

Jessica paused suddenly, her ears twitching. The forest around them had gone still—no birdsong, no rustling in the undergrowth. Even the wind seemed reluctant to blow through the branches. A single fat raindrop landed on her ear.

She lowered her head to the ground, sniffing intently. A faint chemical smell clung to the leaf litter. Another drop landed next to her. She was running out of time.

Jessica followed the smell and found a tranquilizer dart, broken and half buried in a large boot print. She raised her head. The undergrowth around them was trampled and broken.

They found the capture site.

And not a moment too soon. A loud rumble, much closer this time, seemed to shake the ground where they stood. The clouds opened up, soaking them to the bone in minutes.

Jessica turned and let out a low chuff to Isaac. He chuffed back in response and took the lead, disappearing into the rain and mist. She followed close behind.

Not far from the capture site they found the road. Deep ruts in the dirt filling with rainwater were the only sign of tire tracks left.

They followed the road, picking their way through the undergrowth. They didn't dare leave the cover of the treeline, even when the brush was too thick to pass through.

Jessica's paws slipped in the wet leaves, her muscles beginning to ache. Each step took more effort than the last. She could hear Isaac panting beside her.

Just when she thought she couldn't possibly go any further, the trees ended. Jessica froze at the treeline. A twelve-foot chain-link fence topped with two feet of barbed wire surrounded an imposing building. The road led to a large gate flanked by guard towers. At least two more towers could be seen peeking out from behind the building.

Jessica crouched low in the undergrowth, rainwater streaming off her pelt. Next to her Isaac did the same. Their eyes met. She gave a soft chuff, then turned away and shifted.

Her joints cracked and twisted, more uncomfortable than painful. Goose bumps popped up as her fur disappeared. Jessica hugged herself. The rain was *freezing*. Her teeth chattered.

Isaac followed a moment later, also replacing fur with goose bumps. Jessica peeked over at him—then froze. Vicious scars marred his chest, pale and brutal against his damp skin. She looked away quickly, guilt and curiosity tangling in her stomach.

"So what's the plan?" he said.

"I go in, find Wyatt, and break him out. And Curtis too," she added quickly.

"How the hell do you plan on getting in there?" Isaac asked incredulously.

"I'll figure something out," Jessica hissed back. She peered down at the fence, then the gate, searching for the solution. An idea was beginning to form. A stupid idea. Stupid enough that it might actually work.

"No, Jess, this is ridic—"

A faint hiss of compressed air was their only warning.

A dart thudded into Isaac's shoulder. Jessica gaped in horror. Isaac clutched at the dart and yanked it out. He peered over at her, his eyes glazing over before they rolled back and he crumpled.

Jessica's vision blurred. She looked down at her arm stupidly, peering at the dart piercing her own skin.

Then the world went dark.

Into the Lion's Den

Dear Diary,

One week left. I'm so nervous.

I just want this to be over. I want to get my test done and get on with my life without all this tension.

Mom and Dad will be happy to be done with it too. The closer we get to the date, the more fluttery and weird Mom gets. And Dad…well he's not much different. A little more irritable, but that's about it.

I can hear Jess coming up the stairs. She's doing that stompy run she does when she has news. I better go.

Love Always,
Dani

~*~

The light above her head was flickering—and it was getting annoying.

Jessica sat at her desk back at school, staring at the blackboard. She was trying to take notes, but every time the light flickered, the notes on the blackboard changed.

Flick. Bullet points outlining the practices of ancient tribes.

Flick. A paragraph on *MacBeth*.

Flick. Math problems.

Jessica rubbed her eyes, temples pounding with a dull, throbbing ache.

Flick. A dissected frog.

Flick. A map of the country.

Flick. A strand of DNA.

Jessica peered at the board. Five spots on the DNA strand were glowing. Light pulsed, burning brighter and brighter until she was sure the board would catch fire.

"Jess."

Jessica turned. Wyatt sat next to her, staring straight ahead, his expression wooden.

"Jess."

Jessica whipped around. Isaac sat on the other side, his face mirroring Wyatt's.

"Subje—responsive." A strange new voice crackled through the PA system.

Jessica whipped her head back to the front. The lights stuttered in a rapid rhythm. The blackboard buzzed, switching between subjects too fast to follow.

"Run."

Jessica turned to peer behind her. She caught a glimpse of Dani jumping out the window, diving into the ocean, and disappearing into its depths. She tried to get up, but found her hands and feet were shackled to the desk.

Then the desk started sinking into the floor.

Jessica watched in horror as her feet disappeared beneath the tile. She screamed and pulled with all her might. It was no good. The shackles were too strong to break, too tight to slip out of. All she could do was struggle as she sank down, down into the darkness—

A gloved hand wrenched open her eye and shone a bright light in it.

Jessica tried to jerk her head away with a cry. A thick leather strap held it in place. She tried to reach up to push the hand away, but found her hands tethered to her sides with strong leather cuffs. She kicked with all her might—only to feel more cuffs biting into her ankles.

"Subject is conscious and is responding to visual stimuli." A bored voice drifted over Jessica's head. She twisted in vain, trying to see who was talking. The leather strap across her forehead held her tight. Her heart pounded against her ribs. Her chest felt tight. Panic crawled up her spine like a spider.

"Auditory stimuli—"

Reeeeeee!

Jessica flinched and yelled as an earsplitting alarm blasted into her ear.

"Auditory stimuli test successful," the voice droned, as if ticking boxes on a checklist.

Heels clicked against the floor, coming closer. A white lab coat flashed in and out of her peripheral vision, but the strap kept her head maddeningly locked in place.

"Tactile response, upper left arm—"

Jessica yelled in pain as something sharp pierced her arm. Her arm jerked instinctively against the restraints.

"Successful. Lower left arm—"

Jessica yelled again.

Each of her limbs were mercilessly tested this way. Each of her fingertips. The bottoms of her feet. Jessica was sobbing, begging them to stop. Her fingers had to be prised open and pinned down as something sharp was jabbed into each tip.

"Subject is fully responsive. Recommend two days surveillance for any adverse effects. Sedation prescribed for transport."

"Wait—" she gasped. "Please—"

No one listened. She was nothing to them. A wrinkled middle-aged woman's face loomed over her—bored and impassive. Cold metal pressed against her neck, followed by a sharp pain. She only had time to gasp before darkness claimed her again.

~*~

Jessica woke slowly, clawing her way to consciousness through the thick fog of sedation. Her mouth was dry. Her limbs ached. Her head was swimming, making her feel dizzy even while lying down.

She finally pulled herself upright with a groan. A dim yellow bulb glowed faintly above her, barely illuminating the small cell. There was no bed, no window, just four dingy white walls and a door with no doorknob.

A faint cough made her jump.

Across the room, a gaunt figure was curled in the corner. She was so pale she nearly blended in with the walls. Her skin was stretched taut over her bones. Thin wisps of white hair grew patchy on her skull.

Jessica covered her mouth in horror as the girl's thin frame arched and convulsed with a coughing fit. She must have gasped, because the girl looked up at her. A smile spread across her emaciated face. A trickle of blood dribbled down the side of her mouth.

It couldn't be.

"Hannah?"

"Dani, you came," Hannah gasped, her eyes glazing over. "You came back for me."

"Hannah, it's Jessica," Jessica whispered, crawling to her. "Do you remember me? Dani's little sister?"

"Of course, I remember her," Hannah rasped. "She's—what's her name again?"

"Jessica," Jessica whispered desperately, "Hannah, it's Jessica. What happened to you?"

"They cured me," Hannah mumbled. "They keep curing me, but it keeps coming back." Her head lolled back down to the floor with a dull *thunk*.

"*Cured* you? What—?" Jessica reeled back as Hannah broke into another coughing fit. Drops of blood scattered across the floor, the deep red stark against the dingy white.

"I don't…I don't think I'm gonna…gonna be able to go with you…Dani," Hannah gasped, her breathing ragged. "You're gonna have to… have to go by…yourself."

"No, no, no, Hannah," Jessica said, frantically pulling Hannah upright. She was featherlight. Her head drooped, like it was too heavy for her neck to support.

Jessica cradled Hannah like a child, resting her head on her shoulder so she could breathe better. Tears blurred her vision as Hannah's breath rasped, shallow in her chest.

"Dani?" Hannah's voice crackled like brittle paper, barely audible.

"Yeah?" Jessica whispered, her voice catching in her throat.

"Did I make it? Am I free?"

Jessica choked back a sob. Tears flowed, unbidden, down her cheeks.

"Yes, Hannah," Jessica whispered, her voice cracking. "You're free. You're free."

Jessica kept repeating it even after Hannah drew her last breath. "You're free."

~*~

Jessica had no way to know how long she was locked in that tiny cell. Guards brought her food periodically. A bowl of extremely watery soup with smelly wilted leaves and chunks of—something whiteish. Or was it yellow? It might have been a potato, except for the taste. A slice of stale bread twice a day. One bottle of water accompanied her first meal. By the time they brought her a second one, she was so thirsty she drank half of it in one gulp.

It was hard, forcing herself to eat that first day. Hannah's body lay in the corner, a glaring reminder of what awaited her if she didn't find a way out. They didn't remove it until her third day—or rather, nine food cycles later. By then, her skin had taken on a waxy yellow-gray pallor. Her limbs, so pitifully thin at the beginning, were swollen. Patches of her paper-thin skin had darkened, mottled purple and green.

As the guards heaved Hannah into a black body bag, something in Jessica cracked. She turned her face to the wall and didn't move until they were gone.

The silence was the worst part. The guards didn't talk to her. They came in pairs, one pointing a gun at her while the other dropped off her food and took away her old tray. Jessica tried everything—yelling, begging, crying, screaming. Once she even tried being funny. Nothing worked. They remained stoic. Silent.

Jessica found herself filling the silence any way she could. She started talking to Hannah's corpse. First, she imagined Hannah's replies, then started *hearing* them. She hummed nonsense tunes, songs she remembered from the radio, jingles from commercials that used to drive her crazy. Anything to keep the silence from swallowing her whole.

Jessica searched the cell obsessively, fingertips tracing every corner, every seam in the concrete, desperate for a flaw she could exploit. The door was metal, solid and heavy. The walls were cement. Someone had started a tally in one corner. Jessica added to it, keeping track of the only thing she could—meals.

~*~

Sixteen meals after Hannah's body was removed, two guards entered, pointing their guns at Jessica. Her breath caught, and she nearly choked. She was picking at her breakfast—a mouldy slice of bread. Clearly, this wasn't a food delivery. What could they possibly—?

"Get up!" one guard barked.

Jessica's eyes widened, and she scrambled to her feet.

"Wha—?" Jessica's question was silenced by a backhand that sent her stumbling back.

"No talking. Walk." The guard grabbed her arm, squeezing just hard enough to be painful. The other guard grabbed her other arm with equal ferocity.

A knot of apprehension settled in her chest. She knew instinctively that danger was waiting for her, but she couldn't do anything but fall in step between the guards.

They led her down a corridor of metal doors. The occasional moan or scream bled into the hall. Each one made Jessica's chest tighten until she felt like she was breathing through a straw. Nausea overwhelmed her, and it took everything she had not to bend over and puke right there in the hall.

After a tense ride in an elevator, Jessica stepped out—and immediately balked.

The room was a blinding white. Six metal gurneys were bolted to the floor, slanted at forty-five-degree angles. They were surrounded by carts of equipment attended by a team of technicians. Two of the gurneys were occupied already, one girl, maybe a few years older than Jessica, and...

Jessica's breath caught in her throat.

Curtis.

He looked smaller. Hollowed out. Pain and grief carved deep lines in his face. A flicker of recognition flashed through his eyes as they met Jessica's, followed by a deep shame. He was strapped down just like the girl beside him, but he hung limp against his restraints.

He was already broken.

Jessica's guards pulled her forward. She dug in her heels, but days of starvation left her no strength for resistance. The guards dragged her past the girl, past Curtis, to the next empty gurney.

"Curt—" Jessica's words were cut off by a blow to her abdomen.

"No talking," her guard intoned as Jessica gasped for breath.

As soon as she was secured, the elevator doors opened again. Another boy, probably Dani's age, was dragged in and strapped in on Jessica's left. Before they got him situated, he managed to bite one of his guards hard enough to draw blood. The guard howled, and the boy earned a blow to the head before he was unceremoniously gagged with a thick piece of leather.

After the boy, another girl, shaking and terrified, was brought in and strapped in without incident.

The elevator opened one last time. Jessica peeked over—and froze. *Isaac.*

Two guards dragged him in, kicking and grunting. His eyes flashed dangerously as he struggled. A leather gag was already secured in his mouth, and he sported a fresh black eye and split lip. Two more guards rushed forward and helped secure Isaac to his gurney.

"Subjects secured. Trial C-926 commencing," a man in a white coat announced.

Jessica finally looked around. Large windows looked down at them from the top of the room. People in white coats sat in rows behind them, observing them with blank expressions. Some held clipboards on their laps, ready to take notes.

"This trial will test two of the latest serums, SE-174 and KD-475," the man droned on. "Each serum will be tested on both a male and female specimen. One set will receive a placebo as a control."

The man gestured. Six technicians stepped forward, each holding a tray bearing an identical syringe. Each syringe bore a serial number.

"Subject 788-8326-PW27 will receive serum TO-4028." A technician stepped up to the first girl. Tears rolled down her face as she pleaded with the tech.

"No...no, please—"

The technician ignored her. The needle jabbed mercilessly into her arm, and the plunger moved steadily down. Jessica could see the people in the gallery above beginning to make notes on their clipboards.

"Subject 947-2749-FC36 will receive serum DS-3759." Another technician stepped up to Curtis and inserted their needle. Curtis barely flinched.

Jessica's stomach churned. She was next.

"Subject 943-3853-HJ28 will receive serum SH-2838."

Jessica pulled feebly at her restraints, desperate to get away, but knowing she couldn't. Her heart pounded in her chest, faster and faster as the technician approached her. An involuntary gasp of pain escaped her lips as the needle entered and emptied its contents into her bloodstream.

"Subject—" The man's next sentence was cut off by a noise to Jessica's right. She whipped her head around just in time to see Curtis jerking and thrashing against his restraints. His back arched so violently she was surprised it didn't break. His eyes rolled back in their sockets. White foam spilled from his mouth.

"Curtis?" Jessica gasped. *"Curtis! Help him! Please—"*

The technicians ignored her screams. A guard roughly gagged her, securing the strip of leather behind her head. A woman in the gallery watched with interest, scribbling notes on her clipboard as fast as her pen would move. Not one of them moved to help.

She watched helplessly as Curtis jerked uncontrollably against his restraints. His lips slowly turned blue beneath the foam. Finally, after what felt like a lifetime, Curtis's body gave one final jerk, then went limp.

"Subject 862-7366-HI58 will—"

Jessica sobbed.

~*~

Jessica was dragged off her gurney and tossed unceremoniously into a small room. A large window into the next room adorned one wall. Two of the scientists from the gallery sat silently, staring at her.

She lay where she landed, too dizzy to move. The fluorescent light buzzed overhead. Her heartbeat pounded in her ears. Her shoulder throbbed where the serum had been injected. She could almost feel it making its way through her, like icy daggers stabbing through her veins.

Jessica forced herself to sit up. Her head swam and the room spun. Nausea gripped her, forced her to crawl to the corner and empty the meager contents of her stomach.

She threw up until she had nothing left. She stood up on unsteady feet and stared through the window. The scientists stared back. They might have been mannequins, except for the occasional twitch of pencil on paper.

"Jess."

Jessica wheeled around. It had been Dani's voice. She was sure of it. But she was alone.

"Jess."

Jessica spun again. Dani's voice was so close. Like she'd been whispering in her ear.

"Jessica."

She turned her head so fast her neck jolted in protest. The scientists behind the glass were gone. In their places stood her parents. They looked the same as they had the day they'd taken Dani for her test.

"Time to go, Jessica."

Her mother's smile was wide, too wide, teeth too sharp. They reached for her, their arms stretching through the glass.

"No! You can't make me! No!" Jessica screamed, pressing herself against the opposite wall.

"What's wrong?"

Jessica's head whipped around.

Curtis was strapped to the gurney next to her. White foam lined his blue lips. His spine twisted. His skin was gray, but his eyes glittered. The straps opened, and he stepped down, advancing on Jessica.

"You let me die."

"No, please—" Jessica begged. She scrambled into the furthest corner, holding her arms up as though Curtis's corpse was going to strike her.

"Jess." Dani's voice echoed through the empty room. Jessica opened her eyes a crack. Curtis was nowhere in sight.

"Dani?" Jessica called.

"Jess."

"Dani!" Jessica went over to the window. There, sitting between the scientists, was Dani. She was soaking wet, seaweed stuck in her hair.

"Dani, help me!" Jessica pleaded, beating her fists against the window. Her sister didn't move. Didn't blink. Didn't breathe.

"Dani!" Jessica screamed.

The room pitched, and she fell to the floor, still screaming for Dani.

The walls pulsed, synced with her heartbeats. Each heartbeat brought the walls in closer, closer, until she was trapped in a tiny box. She sobbed, each breath a chore. The box squeezed smaller and smaller, pressing her legs into her chest.

"Dani—" Jessica gasped. Then her vision swam and darkness engulfed her.

~*~

Jessica woke slowly, blinking up at the fluorescent lights. Her skin was clammy with sweat, and her body trembled violently. For a moment, she refused to move, not sure if she was still hallucinating. She could still hear Dani's voice, faintly echoing through the corners of her mind. The ceiling spun in a slow circle, and it felt like she was on a boat, rocking in the waves.

She closed her eyes and took a few deep, steadying breaths. She could smell the drying vomit in the corner. She could hear the buzz of the lights. Her throat burned, probably from puking. And screaming. Her head throbbed. Her limbs ached.

The pain anchored her. Pulled her back to reality.

The door to the room scraped open loudly, and Jessica scrambled to her feet. She swayed, unsteady, but stayed upright.

Two guards entered. Jessica backed away from them, already trembling. They couldn't possibly be taking her for another test.

Please, God, not again.

The guards grabbed her arms, dragging her from the room without a word. They pulled her down another hallway until they reached a steel door. Unlike the others, this one bore a placard: "Dr. I. Volkov, CEO."

The guards knocked.

"Enter."

The guards pulled Jessica through the door and deposited her in a large leather chair in front of an antique desk. A woman in a tailored white lab coat sat, studying Jessica intently.

Jessica froze. She went cold all over as she gaped at the woman across from her.

No.

It couldn't be.

Irina.

Until the End

Dear Jess,

If you're reading this, that means the worst has happened. I'm a Shifter.

If that is true — if Mom and Dad came home and I'm not with them — find my diary before they do. I hid it in the vent at the back of my closet. I want you to keep it. Read it. Learn from it.

And if you do end up sharing my fate, do not *wait to get tested. Run.*

I love you. Remember that. Shifter or not, I love you.

Love Always,
Dani

~*~

Jessica stared in disbelief.

Irina.

The doctor.

She didn't just work for the SRC. She was the CEO.

Irina studied her, a small smile playing on her lips.

"I must say, Jessica, I am impressed," she said.

Jessica blinked. "I—what?"

"I have been going through the file of the study you were just part of." Irina flicked open a folder in front of her. "Four Shifters received trial serums, two a placebo. Of those who received the serum, you were the only survivor."

"No—" Jessica breathed. Curtis's lifeless body hanging from his restraints flashed before her eyes, and she blinked away tears.

Please, not Isaac too.

Irina flicked to another page. "Yes, it says here one seized on the table—probably an allergic reaction. Unfortunate." She looked up at the horrified look on Jessica's face.

"You—you're a monster," Jessica choked.

Irina didn't look angry, as Jessica would have assumed. In fact, she looked mildly amused.

"*I'm* a monster?" she asked. "My dear, if I am a monster, what does that make you?"

"Me? What are you talking about?" Jessica shot back, anger rising. "I've never—"

"Never what, dear?" Irina asked, amused. "Never killed anyone? We both know that's a lie."

Jessica blanched. "That was different. I wasn't torturing people!"

"No, you just ripped the throat out of a young man, who by the way will now never get to meet his son."

Guilt dropped to the pit of her stomach like a stone. Jessica clenched her jaw shut and balled her hands into fists. Her nails dug into her hands.

"What we are doing here will benefit Shifters and Normals alike in the long run," Irina said, her expression softening into pity. "When we develop the vaccine, our society will be *whole*. No one in the ghetto. No one forced from their homes."

Jessica squirmed as the weight of Irina's words settled. A tiny part of her, the part that still wanted to go home, wanted desperately to believe her.

Irina pounced at Jessica's hesitation, sensing weakness. She stood and moved slowly around the desk, almost predator-like.

"Think of it, Jessica," she continued gently, cajolingly. "No more fear. No more hiding. You could live the life you want. Your *children* could live the lives they want. You could have your family again." Irina held out a hand for Jessica.

Jessica stared at the hand offered to her. A tremor ran through her fingers. The idea of peace—of normalcy—called to that small child deep inside of her. The one that was weary and homesick and longed for her family. Jessica placed her hand in Irina's

Family.

Her parents had a terrible definition of the word. Dani was gone. Who was left?

One by one their faces floated by her mind's eye.

Cassie with her gentle understanding.

Heather's quick wit.

Tia's overprotective temper.

Isaac. Ashley. Sarah. Nathan. Song. Chan-seong.

Wyatt.

Jessica looked up at Irina.

"I *have* a family."

Then she spat directly in Irina's face.

~*~

For thirty whole seconds, neither of them moved.

Jessica watched as Irina's face slowly moved between shock and anger. She took a measured breath and wiped the spittle from her face.

Just as she opened her mouth, a shrill alarm pierced the air. A red light flashed in the hall. Irina's hand froze, mid-wipe.

Jessica took her chance. She lunged.

Irina barely had time to gasp before Jessica connected with her, dragging her to the floor. Jessica straddled her, hitting her with a flurry of fists, taking every ounce of rage she'd ever felt out on the woman under her. She didn't even stop when Irina went still.

A shout from the hallway brought Jessica back to the present. She jumped up and looked around wildly. The file still sat open on Irina's desk. Jessica slammed it shut, grabbed it, and bolted out the door.

If nothing else, it told them how Curtis died.

The hall beyond was chaos. Shouts echoed, boots pounded on linoleum. Jessica duck behind an abandoned cart as two guards sprinted past.

Jessica dashed down the hall, praying she was going the right way. She skidded to a stop as hushed voices drifted from around the corner.

"Kind of bullshit intel is that?" a male voice hissed angrily.

"I told you everything I know, I promise!" a desperate female voice answered.

Jessica's heart dropped to her feet. She recognized that voice.

She peered slowly around the corner. A guard stood with his back to her. His arms were crossed, his stance menacing. Standing in front of the guard, pleading and trembling, was Ashley!

"My brother died in that bogus ambush you set up," the guard said, poking Ashley in the chest. "Now you want me to believe that they aren't planning any rescue? Bullshit."

Jessica's mouth went dry.

Ashley.

Betrayal roiled in her gut, hot and nauseating.

Ashley. Set up the ambush. The one where Curtis was captured... where *Wyatt* was captured.

That fucking *bitch*.

Jessica shook as rage overtook her. She didn't think—she saw the baton hanging loose in the guard's hand and instinct took over. She lunged for it, disarming him before he knew she was there. In one swift move, she swung as hard as she could and connected with the guard's temple. He crumpled to the ground.

A look of relief crossed Ashley's face, then it was replaced by fear as Jessica raised the baton again.

"Jess, thank God you—"

Jessica cut her off. "*You*," she snarled. "You set us up."

Ashley went white. "Jess, it's not—"

"You don't speak," Jessica growled. "Curtis is dead—because of *you*."

Ashley's mouth opened and closed several times. Tears welled in her eyes.

"You don't understand," Ashley pleaded. "They hav—"

"You. Don't. *Speak*!" Jessica roared, swinging the baton. It connected with her temple with a loud *crack!* Ashley crumpled to the ground beside the guard.

~*~

Jessica left the two where they fell, but not before relieving the guard of his key card and gun. She bolted up the hall, swiping the card at the locks as she went. One by one the locks clicked open. Prisoners staggered out hesitantly at first. They were pale, bruised, starved. Some clung to the walls to stay upright.

Not all made it out. Some lay limp on the floor, already dead. Some were too far gone and had to be left behind.

But those who could followed.

When they met the guards, they didn't hesitate. They swarmed them—ragged, furious, united. Batons and guns were ripped from stunned hands.

The prisoners remembered which guards had been cruel. They didn't stand a chance.

Jessica rounded a corner and nearly crashed into someone sprinting toward her. She raised her stolen gun instinctively, clutching the stolen folder to her chest.

"Whoa—Jess, it's me!"

Jessica froze.

"Isaac?" she asked softly, not daring to believe her own eyes.

He nodded, trying to smile and wincing instead. He was limping, bloodied, and wild-eyed. But he was alive.

A rush of relief hit her so hard she nearly collapsed.

"You're not dead," she gasped. It was the only thing she could think to say.

"Uh, no, not since I checked last," Isaac said, looking down at his battered body. "Look, the guards are starting to lock down the prisoner wings. If we want to get out of here, we need to go *now*."

Jessica hesitated. She had to find Wyatt. But where would she even start looking?

"You go ahead," she said firmly. "There's…someone I need to find."

"I'll go with you," he said quickly.

She shook her head. "You need to help them. Go," she urged.

Isaac hesitated. For a heartbeat, it looked like he wanted to argue. Then, before she could say anything, he leaned down and kissed her.

Her eyes widened and a thrill fluttered through her chest.

When they parted, she stared at him, stunned. "Wha—?"

"In case I don't see you again," Isaac murmured.

And then he was gone, ushering the weaker prisoners toward the exits.

~*~

Jessica rushed the opposite direction, unlocking doors as she went. The alarm still blared, a shrill, ceaseless wail that drilled straight through her skull.

Just as she was about to give up hope, she found him.

The very last door at the end of the hall swung open—and there he was. Wyatt, huddled next to a girl that didn't move.

"Wyatt," Jessica breathed, dropping down in front of him. An angry red brand stuck out on his neck—not the triangular Shifter brand. An upside-down *T.* The mark of a traitor.

"She's dead," Wyatt croaked, his eyes distant—haunted.

Jessica looked down at the girl next to them. Her skeletal limbs were beginning to bloat the way Hannah's had. Her skin had the same yellow-gray hue.

"Oh, Wyatt." Jessica's throat clenched, tears pricking her eyes.

"There was nothing I could do. They wouldn't help," Wyatt rasped, hugging his knees tighter. He was shaking.

"I know," Jessica murmured. She wanted to hold him, to help him through this, but they didn't have time. "Trust me, I know. But Wyatt—we have to go. We have to get out of here."

Wyatt blinked, his gaze finally focusing on Jessica. "Jess?" His voice was hesitant, like he wasn't sure it was truly her.

"Yes, Wyatt, it's me. I'm here," Jessica urged. "Please, Wyatt, get up. We have to go."

Jessica managed to get him to his feet. He leaned heavily on her, weak and shaking.

They staggered down the hall. The door to the yard stood ajar, ripped off its hinges by something massive.

They were nearly out. Jess could feel the breeze on her face. She quickened her pace, urging Wyatt forward.

Jessica screamed as she was yanked off her feet. She and Wyatt crashed to the ground in a tangled heap.

A massive snake—six feet long and as thick as her thighs—had her legs wrapped tightly in its body. It was Ashley. It had to be. Her feet were already beginning to lose feeling. She kicked and writhed, but it only squeezed tighter.

She tried to shift. Tried to call the jaguar to her. She had to protect herself. She had to protect Wyatt.

Nothing happened.

The snake slithered higher, wrapping around her torso. She screamed as it squeezed her ribs—*crack!* Something broke.

She gasped and tried to pry the snake loose. She couldn't breathe. She lost more air with every second. Wyatt tried prying the reptile off. The snake struck at him and hissed, sending him stumbling backward.

Black spots danced at the edge of her vision.

A roar—loud, angry, primal—echoed through Jessica's head. She was hallucinating again. She had to be. A big cat leapt over her and slammed into the snake. Two-inch canines sunk into the reptile's skull with a sickening *crunch!*

Jessica gasped as air flooded back into her lungs. Every breath was agony. Her ribs were on fire.

Isaac, now human again, crouched beside her.

"C'mon," he said, gently pulling her upright.

Together the three of them limped out the door.

Behind them, the snake slowly shriveled and twisted. The tail split into legs. Arms sprouted from its sides. In moments, the snake's body was replaced with Ashley's. Her lifeless eyes grew dull as the sun dipped below the treeline.

~*~

The yard was utter chaos. Guards shouted. Animals roared. Two wolves, white and black, wove in unison, snapping at the guards who tried to stop the fleeing prisoners. An owl and an osprey dove at their heads, screeching and raking their faces with their talons. A furious grizzly bear bowled through them, ripping them to shreds.

Jessica half-stumbled, half-dragged Wyatt toward the breach in the fence, file still clasped tightly to her chest. Isaac flanked her, one arm around her waist, supporting her weight.

"Almost there!" he shouted.

A bullet shot past them, just missing Isaac's ear.

The three turned. A guard stood, not far away, gun pointed at Jessica's chest. For a moment the world stilled.

The guard took a step toward them.

"Vermin." He hissed his finger trembling on the trigger. "You're all vermin. You—"

His speech was cut off by a roar. The guard turned just in time to see Ben, all eight hundred grizzly pounds of him, barreling toward him. The guard panicked and shot at him, but the shot went wide, and Ben knocked him aside like he was a rag doll. He hit the ground and didn't get back up.

Jessica gasped, a smile trying to break through the panic—

Crack!

Another gunshot.

Ben fell, collapsing in slow motion.

"No!" Jessica shrieked.

She tore away from Wyatt, from Isaac, her pain forgotten. She dropped to her knees beside the enormous bear, her fingers trembling as she reached for him.

"Ben? *Ben!*"

His breathing was already shallow, ragged. His eyes blinked slowly, unfocused. Then he let out one last, weary *whumph*, and his breathing stopped altogether.

Jessica let out a sound that was half scream, half sob. She buried her face in his thick fur.

He had been her first friend—her first ally in this shitty life she got stuck with.

And now he was gone.

~*~

"Jess, we have to go."

Wyatt placed a gentle hand on her shoulder. She pulled away. She wouldn't leave Ben here. She *couldn't* leave Ben here.

Isaac glanced around nervously. The guards were beginning to regroup. A howl rose through the air. A black wolf snapped furiously, snarling protectively over his injured mate. The owl and the osprey wheeled overhead, more cautious about getting close.

"Do you think you can get her out?" Isaac asked Wyatt.

Wyatt nodded.

Isaac turned and sprinted back into the fray, shifting mid-stride.

"Jess, please," Wyatt said softly, crouching beside her.

Jessica didn't move. Her hands were still tangled in Ben's fur, sticky with blood. Tears streaked down her face. Every sob was a knife in her side, but she couldn't seem to stop.

"He wouldn't want you to die here," Wyatt urged gently.

Jessica squeezed her eyes shut. He was right. She placed a kiss on the bear's snout. Then she turned and took Wyatt's hand. He hauled her gently to her feet, and together they limped through the fence and toward freedom.

~*~

Jessica couldn't recall in the days that followed, how she and Wyatt managed to pick their way through the forest as battered and weak as they were. They arrived back at the warehouse, exhausted and half-starved. Jessica still carried the file she'd stolen from Irina's desk. She handed it over to Heather without a word. She would know what to do with it.

She spent the next three days curled up on her cot. Grief gnawed at her until she was hollow. Her ribs ached constantly, and bruises marred her torso. But the grief hurt worse than all of it.

Wyatt stayed close, bringing her food and forcing her to eat. To drink. To live. On the fourth day, he coaxed her out of her cot.

"C'mon," he said softly. "Let's go outside. Just for a bit."

Jessica didn't want to go outside. She didn't want to move. Her chest was heavy, tight, painful. It weighed her down, and she wasn't sure it would ever go away. Wyatt held out his hand. He didn't push, didn't insist. Just waited.

She forced herself up.

The morning air was sharp and cool as they stepped out the back door of the warehouse. Mist curled around the trunks of the trees. Birds twittered in the canopy. She felt something loosen in her chest. Just a little bit.

They stood in silence for a long time.

"We could still do it, y'know," Wyatt said suddenly.

Jessica turned her head.

"Run away. Just the two of us. Like we planned. Before all this."

Her throat tightened. "Wyatt—"

"I'm serious. We're alive. We're free. There's nothing stopping us."

Jessica closed her eyes. She tried to imagine it. Leaving with Wyatt, knowing what she knew now. Living her life.

She shook her head.

"I can't," she whispered.

Wyatt didn't speak, but he didn't look surprised.

"They're still doing it," Jessica said, voice hoarse. "Still testing, still torturing people. I can't leave knowing it's still happening."

Wyatt exhaled slowly and rubbed the back of his neck. "I was afraid you'd say that."

"Are you mad?"

"No," he said after a beat. "Just—scared, I guess."

Jessica turned toward him. "You can still go. You don't have to—"

"I'm not leaving you," Wyatt said, cutting her off. "I almost lost you once. I won't do it again."

His fingers brushed hers. She didn't pull away.

"This is my fight now too," he said quietly. "Whatever comes next— I'm with you."

Jessica swallowed hard, blinking back tears. For the first time in days, she felt something flicker in her chest that wasn't grief.

Hope.

EPILOGUE

A Stormy Return

Choppy gray waves pounded the shoreline near the Outreach warehouse. The sky was black as ink, moon and stars veiled by massive storm clouds. The wind howled inland through the trees, drowning out all other sounds. Rain came down in torrents.

Nearly a mile offshore a pod of orcas surfaced. They called to each other, their clicks and whines barely audible over the storm. A smaller orca with a damaged fluke pulled away from the others, clicking out a farewell.

The orca barreled for the shore, letting the waves pull her closer and closer to the beach. With one final surge of power, the orca beached itself. Cries of alarm drifted in from her companions.

The orca let out a soft, strangled whine. Slowly, it shrank—collapsing inward, reshaping—until a young woman knelt in its place. Her black hair was matted with sand and seawater. Naked, trembling, she rose to her feet.

She took one shaky step. Stumbled. Fell.

She rose again. Stumbled. Fell.

Two more times she stood and stumbled before she found her balance. Shaking rainwater out of her eyes, she limped up the beach toward the warehouse. One of her feet, the same as her damaged fluke, was twisted and mangled.

As the door to the warehouse swung open, the guard on duty gasped.

It was impossible.

She couldn't be.

Jessica pulled her sister—her actual, real, live sister—into a hug, screaming.

"Dani!"